A kiss for the Sheriff

Book One

Small Town Matchmaker

Cheryl Wright

A Kiss for the Sheriff
(Book One, Small Town Matchmaker)

Copyright 2023 by Cheryl Wright

Small Town Romance Publications

To Margaret Tanner, my very dear friend and fellow author, for her enduring encouragement and friendship.

To Alan, my husband of over forty-eight years, who has been a relentless supporter of my writing and dreams for many years.

To You, my wonderful readers, who encourage me to continue writing these stories. It is such a joy knowing so many of you enjoy reading my stories as much as I love writing them for you.

Table of Contents

Chapter One

Crystal Springs, Montana – 1880s

"Aw, come on, Harley. Why do you have to make it so difficult?" Sheriff Wyatt Holt shoved Harley Jones into a cell and slammed the door closed. When he wasn't drunk, Harley was an upstanding citizen. It was a pity he was drunk more often than he wasn't.

Wyatt turned and headed to his desk. More paperwork. Lately it felt like sorting through endless red tape was his job rather than keeping the peace in Crystal Springs.

He glanced up as the door opened and his deputy entered with another drunk for the cells. "The saloon is out of hand," Deputy Tommy Garrett said. "It's getting rowdy over there."

Wyatt sighed. He knew Crystal Springs was quiet when he agreed to transfer here around two years ago—quiet was what he liked. Especially after all his years as a sheriff. Drunks were not his favorite people to deal with, but it was far better than gun-wielding bandits. The town had seen its fair share of those over the years, but thankfully, not lately. That was long before his time, and for that, Wyatt was grateful.

"I suppose I have to arrange food for those two varmints," Wyatt said, more to himself than his deputy. He sighed then and stood. "This one is ready for the file." He handed over the form he'd just completed and walked out the door.

The fresh air hit him in the face, effectively waking Wyatt up. He didn't mind being inside, provided he got to go outside now and then. At least the previous sheriff had set up a routine—doing rounds every night was a simple task, but also provided Wyatt with an opportunity to take in the fresh air, as well as stretch his legs.

Across the road was the mercantile. He probably needed to pay a visit there. Stores were low, and he needed to eat. Not that he was much of a cook. More often than not, he ate at the diner.

Wyatt was a newcomer to the town. He wasn't really, but in the scheme of things, according to the townsfolk, he was. If you weren't born there, you were a newcomer.

He didn't mind what label they put on him, provided they didn't break the law. Mostly, the sheriff's office dealt with drunks, but now and then, Wyatt and his deputy were chasing cattle rustlers. They'd had to intervene in a feud or two, as well as petty theft, but apart from that, he led a fairly quiet life in Crystal Springs.

It was exactly what he'd signed up for.

Wyatt had been enticed into becoming a sheriff at the young age of twenty-five. That was far too long ago for him to want to remember. Already past his fortieth birthday, a quiet town like this one was where he wanted to retire. He was good for a few more years yet as town sheriff. After that? He honestly wasn't sure.

He wasn't one for gardening, and he only visited the saloon to drag the drunks away. He'd pondered the problem before, and still hadn't come up with a viable solution.

As an unmarried man, it would be a lonely life, no matter what he did in retirement.

"Good afternoon, Wyatt."

Wyatt glanced across the road to see Beth staring at him. She waved and his heart fluttered. Elizabeth Hughes, or Beth, as most folks called her, owned the diner. He'd spent many a time there eating her delicious meals.

He'd been warned the town had a matchmaker, and it kept him on alert. Lucky for Wyatt, most of the women in Crystal Springs were far too young for him. In most cases, he was old enough to be their father. That had kept him safe.

Beth was another situation altogether. He liked her—a lot. But Beth had no time for suitors.

Sure, she invited him to supper now and then—on the days the diner was quiet. According to Tommy, his deputy, she had far more invitations than most, but he didn't believe that was true. "Afternoon, Beth," he called back, then headed for the mercantile. Not knowing what he wanted for supper made it difficult to know what to buy.

Beth went into the mercantile moments before he did.

"We have two guests at the jailhouse," he said, and Beth nodded. They'd done this several times before over the past two years. She immediately understood he needed her to supply the prisoners' meals tonight and in the morning.

Moments later, he began to wander aimlessly, checking out the supplies, then reached for a can of beans. Maybe he'd grab several while he was there. It would save him a trip some other time. Wyatt headed to the counter. "Do you have any sausages?" he asked the store owner. "Oh, and eggs too."

"Wyatt Holt, you are not having beans for supper!" Beth sounded exasperated. "There is room for one more at the diner."

"I can't…"

"You most certainly can," Beth insisted. "I'll expect you for supper at the diner. Six-thirty—don't be late." She picked up her groceries, huffed, and hurried out of the store.

"She likes you," Dennis, the store owner, said, then held up one can. "Do you still want the beans?" He laughed then, and Wyatt scowled. Since when did Beth like him? They were friends. Had been from the moment he'd arrived.

Beth was like that. She liked everyone, and everyone liked her. She was a sweet person who would do anything for anyone. More often than not, she did.

Like invite Wyatt to supper. It wasn't the first time she'd invited him, either. That gave him pause, and Wyatt wondered if Dennis was right. Perhaps Beth did like him.

"Yes, I want the beans," he said, scowling. "I'll take a half dozen eggs and six sausages too. Oh, and a loaf of bread." Wyatt left in a huff the moment his purchases were bagged and noted in the account book. Since when did Dennis become the town matchmaker? He hurried back to the sheriff's residence and put his purchases away. He cleaned himself up and, despite his reluctance, prepared to visit Beth's diner for supper.

It was a quiet night for the diner, as Wyatt knew it would be. Friday and Saturday nights were Beth's busiest nights—he knew that from experience and avoided going there on those nights. He was someone who liked to keep to himself, but the townsfolk liked to socialize and would visit his table. Wyatt simply wanted a good home-cooked meal, not all the trappings that went with it.

As he headed toward the diner, he halted. Beth was friendly, and had invited him to the diner a few times now. In truth, it should be the other way around. Wyatt should be inviting her out, but short of taking her to one of the outlying towns, he had nowhere to take her. He couldn't very well invite her to supper at her own diner, could he?

He shook his head. Should he even go there? What if Beth expected far more than friendship? As sheriff, it wasn't something he pursued. Besides, he wasn't young anymore. Forty was but a distant memory, and Beth wasn't far behind him, although she was yet to hit that milestone.

Still, provided they kept it platonic, he would be happy. Beth had long been a widow and had no children. Apart from running the diner, she was a free agent.

"Sheriff!" Beth's voice rang out down the road. Did that mean the diner was empty? He wasn't sure that was a good option. Being alone with Beth was not what he'd counted on.

Wyatt lifted an arm and waved. Shudders went through him at the sight of her. For what reason, he did not know.

"I apologize," he said when he got closer. "I had to store my purchases before I could leave."

She reached out and cupped his hands with both of hers. Her hands were tiny, but her touch sent shivers down his spine. If he hadn't thought it rude, Wyatt would have turned around that very moment and gone back home. The thought of sausages and beans for supper wasn't exactly appealing, but neither did he want to give this wonderful lady the wrong impression.

She dropped her hands and waved away his concerns. "It's nothing," she said. "Come on inside. Supper is almost ready."

As they went in, he noticed the *closed* sign on the door. It must be Tuesday. The diner was closed Tuesdays as it was so quiet. Why hadn't he realized that before accepting her invitation? It meant they would be completely alone. It wasn't something Wyatt relished.

In some ways, he did. Beth was beautiful, and an excellent cook. He simply didn't want to lead her on and let her think he was interested in courting her. Or marriage.

Neither was something he was willing to pursue.

Chapter Two

"Sit down. Make yourself comfortable." Beth could see the sheriff's discomfort from the moment she held his hands. Almost immediately, she let go. The last thing she wanted to do was make him feel ill at ease.

They'd been friends for around two years now—almost since the moment he arrived in town. Wyatt had been a sheriff for a very long time, even longer than Beth had been married. If her husband hadn't died suddenly some years ago, she would still be married to her childhood sweetheart.

The memory made her choke up. Luckily, she was in the kitchen and not sitting with her guest. "It's nothing special," Beth announced as approached the table.

Wyatt glanced down at the food she placed in front of him. "It looks pretty special to me," he said, then grinned. "I haven't had steak since the last time I was here."

As she sat opposite him, Beth reached for his hand. She bowed her head and Wyatt followed her lead. Then she said a prayer of thanks.

Beth reluctantly let go of his hand. For some silly reason, she felt comfort touching him. She had that same feeling the last time he ate there. Wyatt sat across the table, looking at her. He might be a world-worn sheriff, but he still had manners. He waited for her to eat before he tucked in.

"This is good," he said. "Not that I expected anything else," he quickly added, then went back to his food.

She studied him. Wyatt was a good man. He looked out for the townsfolk and was a kind-hearted person. There was little in the way of criminal activity in Crystal Springs, and that was what made it so appealing.

The stage went through once a week, but it was mostly locals who alighted there. They got the occasional visitor, but that was it. It was the perfect place to live. At least to Beth's mind.

"That was delicious, as always," Wyatt said, as he wiped his mouth with a napkin. He reached out and took a sip of coffee. Beth caught him studying her over the top of his mug. It made her smile.

Their new sheriff, who had been here for quite some time now, mostly kept to himself unless it was necessary. That wasn't always a good thing. In Beth's mind, anyway. It made it extremely difficult to know what he was thinking.

She stood and gathered up the soiled dishes. Wyatt began to stand. "Stay there and enjoy your coffee. I'll be back shortly." She hurried out to the kitchen and cut the apple pie she'd made earlier, placing a slice in each bowl. She cut Wyatt's far larger than her own, knowing he was a big eater. She added a large blob of clotted cream to each, then headed back to their table.

Wyatt stared down into the bowl as it was placed in front of him. "This is too much, Beth," he said, but lifted his spoon, then waited for her to eat.

She smiled at him. "You'll manage," she said, then chuckled.

"You truly are the best cook in town," he told her, and Beth knew he believed every word.

"Thank you for a wonderful meal," Wyatt said, as he stood some time later. "I have to do my rounds. Did you…" He paused, thought for a moment, then began again. "Would you care to join me? We can walk off that delicious meal." He laughed then, and it lit up his face. It wasn't often Beth saw him laugh. In his job, she could understand why.

"That would be nice. I'll just grab a shawl." It wasn't cold, but the air had a chill this time of night.

She returned a short time later and wondered if she was doing the right thing. They were friends, and that was how they should remain.

Wyatt opened the door, and Beth locked it behind them. In the light of the full moon, they headed down Main Road, strolling along the boardwalk. Wyatt stopped at every building, checked the door was locked, and peered inside. This was a first for Beth. He had never asked her to accompany him before. Simply being in his company filled her with joy. It had always been that way.

When they arrived at the mercantile, the door was unlocked. Wyatt pushed Beth behind him. "Stay here," he said firmly, then strode inside. A shudder went through her. Beth wasn't sure if it was because he was protective of her, or for another reason entirely.

It wasn't long before he returned. "It's alright. Dennis is in the storeroom, and forgot to lock the door when the store closed." She breathed a sigh of relief. It could have been an entirely different outcome. She shuddered to think how that could have turned out. Wyatt could have been hurt, or worse. She didn't want to think about it.

It apparently hadn't bothered Wyatt one iota. The next thing she knew, he put an arm around her waist and led Beth to the next building. She was getting far too used to his touch, but Beth wasn't certain what to do about it. Nor was she certain she wanted to have him stop. That thought bothered her even more.

As they moved to the next building, she shivered. Troubling thoughts ran through her mind once again. What if there really was a break-in? Would something terrible happen to Wyatt? It was then Beth realized it was the reason he kept his distance from people, women in particular. She'd already lost one husband and knew the heartache that brought. She was not prepared to go through that again.

Not that Wyatt had proposed such a thing. She was certainly getting ahead of herself. "Are you cold?" Wyatt asked, glancing across at her.

She shook her head, then realized he may not see it in the semi-darkness. "Not cold. I worry about your safety." Beth heard the emotion in her own voice and wondered what that was about. They'd become friends, nothing more. She expected things to stay that way.

Wyatt chuckled. "Nothing ever happens around here, you know that. We are so out of the way, and the lawmen here are crazy." He grinned then. "Criminals avoid us like the plague."

His words made Beth laugh. She'd not seen this side of Wyatt before. But she knew he was right. There was little in the way of criminal activity. Apart from a few cattle rustlers and teenagers getting up to mischief, drunks at the saloon were the worst he'd encountered since arriving.

He'd told her previously, keeping the peace is what he liked best, and that's what he did most of the time. Apart from paperwork. Wyatt was always bemoaning the amount of paperwork he had to complete with even the smallest misdemeanour. Putting a teenager behind bars for even an hour could land him in hot water without the corresponding report.

Beth glanced up at him. Wyatt was a big man, at over six feet. She felt protected when he was around. Not that she particularly felt unsafe, but it was difficult to explain. She didn't understand it herself. Suddenly, she noticed him staring at her in the moonlight. His eyes sparkled, and she wondered if hers did the same.

"Beth," he whispered, then leaned in until she felt his breath against her lips.

He hesitated, and she wondered if he was unsure that he wanted to kiss her, or if he was waiting for permission to go ahead. She stared into his eyes, then, without thinking, reached up and cupped his face with her hands.

Then she kissed him.

Chapter Three

Wyatt revelled in the feel of Beth's lips. After all the time they'd known each other, all the times he'd longed to hold her, to kiss her, never had he given into his feelings.

Neither of them were spring chickens, and it seemed absurd to feel this way. Being on the wrong side of forty, he truly believed he was beyond the age any woman would be interested in him.

Did that mean he was wrong?

The pair had been friends since he'd arrived in town. Over those two years, they'd become nothing more. Now he wasn't clear if that was because of his reluctance, or whether it wasn't meant to be. Staring into her face now, Beth appeared to be glowing. That could be the moonlight, or it could be something else entirely.

He might have originally instigated the kiss, but when he'd hesitated, it was Beth who took it to the next level. His reluctance was out of respect for her as his friend. They'd never walked alone in the dark before. When he'd eaten at the diner before, other patrons had been there as well. That meant they weren't alone as they were tonight.

Now he wondered if Beth was testing the waters, so to speak, to find out if they were suited. He'd always thought they were, but still kept his distance. He didn't want to complicate their friendship, but now it was too late for that.

Besides, far too many of his lawmen friends had ended up in an early grave, leaving grieving wives and children behind.

He was certain Beth did not plan on being a two-time widow. Her husband was long gone, but it seemed she still grieved him.

Without thinking about what he was doing, Wyatt pulled Beth close and wrapped his arms around her. It felt so good to hold her like this. Beth didn't complain, and instead, leaned into him. Then he heard her sigh. Wyatt's heart pounded. If things didn't work out between them, would that leave their friendship in tatters? Wyatt didn't want to think about that possibility. Instead, he delighted in holding her in his arms.

Without warning, Beth pulled back. He watched as she ran her fingers through her hair, then straightened her skirts. She glanced up at him, her cheeks rosy with embarrassment. "I'm sorry, Wyatt," she said cautiously. "I don't know what came over me." She turned then and appeared about to run. He reached out and grabbed her arm.

Beth stared at him and then his hand where he held her. He immediately dropped his hand. "No, I'm sorry," he said. "It's entirely my fault. If I hadn't started it…"

She pursed her lips and put her hands on her hips. "I guess we're both to blame," she said, ending the sentence with a sigh. "We'll just have to make sure it never happens again."

Wyatt wasn't sure he wanted that. He enjoyed having Beth's lips on his. And he sure liked it when his arms were wrapped around her. She'd held him so tight, Wyatt was convinced she'd liked it too.

"Perhaps…" He'd intended to ask *what if he didn't want that*, but thought better of it. Beth was a widow, after all. An upstanding citizen of Crystal Springs. She couldn't afford to get caught up in a scandal. If the town gossips found out about them, they would spread it far and wide.

Then it hit him. There was no 'them'. He and Beth were not together, and there was nothing for anyone to spread. He straightened his shoulders, hooked his arm through Beth's, and continued on his rounds with his wonderful friend beside him.

Wyatt lay in bed.

The moon glowed through the bedroom window, keeping him awake. Only Wyatt knew it wasn't the moonlight keeping him awake, but that kiss. The one Beth had planted on his lips earlier in the night.

Despite her objections, Wyatt knew it was all his fault. He should have known better than to ask Beth to accompany him on his rounds.

All this time, he'd had feelings for her. He knew and did nothing about it out of respect. The fact she was a widow made it more difficult. He was sure she would be conflicted over a new relationship, whether that was with him or someone else entirely. Her husband had been gone for years now, and according to others, she'd been alone ever since. He'd respected her decision to keep things that way.

Until tonight.

Wyatt wasn't sure if he was caught up in the moment, whether the moonlight was a factor, or whether his concern for her after finding the mercantile unlocked played a factor.

Or perhaps it was none of those.

He sat on the side of the bed. It must be close to dawn, and he'd dozed a few times, but that was it. Resigned to the fact he wouldn't sleep, he wanted coffee. Wyatt would rather be fully awake than partially asleep. Strong coffee was definitely what he needed. Then he would go for a stroll around town. The brisk morning air would shake him fully awake.

He pulled on his pants and shirt, and secured his sheriff's badge. Then he headed to the tiny kitchen that came with the cottage. He almost didn't accept the free accommodation—the cottage was tiny, and he was used to something far bigger. But Crystal Springs was not huge, and he should be grateful for small mercies.

When he retired, he would take the money he'd saved from not having to pay for somewhere to live, and would buy a house. He might even build something out of town.

The house he built would be big enough to accommodate both Wyatt and a wife.

He slammed his coffee down on the small kitchen table. Coffee ended up across the table, and there was little of it left in the metal mug. He gave a low growl.

None of these thoughts had crossed his mind until now. His fingers went to his lips. Beth had a lot to answer for. He might have leaned in to kiss her, but he'd held back. She was the one who finished what he had started. Even as he backed off, she'd grabbed his face and kissed him.

Now he couldn't stop thinking about the petite diner owner. The widow who was off limits.

He grabbed a cloth and cleaned up the contents of his coffee mug. Brushing his hair back off his face with his fingers, Wyatt headed to the bathroom. A splash of cold water on his face would bring back his senses. At least he hoped it would.

He stared at his reflection in the mirror. It was not a good idea—dark circles under his eyes showed the world he hadn't slept well. It made him wonder if Beth had slept better than he had.

Wyatt vowed to keep away from the diner today. He would keep his distance from Beth, not only today, but for the rest of his time here in town.

The trouble was, the feel of her lips was ingrained on his. Besides, she was an excellent cook, and he liked her company. He was in a genuine dilemma and didn't know how to move forward.

He stormed out of the cottage and strolled around town. It was what he needed. The chilly morning air hit him in the face, and Wyatt pulled up the collar of his heavy coat. It wasn't winter, but the mornings were still brisk and a little chilly.

He didn't normally do morning rounds, but today was an exception. He would rather keep busy than sit on the side of the bed and bemoan his situation. He only hoped he didn't come across Beth on his travels.

Except Wyatt knew that wasn't true. He adored spending time with the beautiful widow, but now their situation was different. Their relationship would be strained after the events of last night. It only took moments, but he had changed their friendship forever.

His stomach rumbled. Wyatt glanced up and saw Joel Evans moving around the bakery. He did not envy the man, having to rise in the darkest part of the night. At the same time, he was thankful. If it wasn't for people like Joel, he wouldn't be able to have breakfast and a decent coffee. He tapped on the door and put his face to the glass.

Joel glanced his way, then waved. The moment the door was opened, delicious aromas assaulted his senses. "That smells amazing," Wyatt said, then grinned.

"Good morning to you, too," Joel said, a grin cutting his face as well. "Grab a table. Let me get you something to eat, Sheriff."

Wyatt winced. No one ever saw him as Wyatt. He would forever be the sheriff, even when he wasn't the sheriff. Although there was an exception—Beth. She was one of the few in town who called him by his actual name. A shiver ran through him when she did it, and now he wondered if the reasons for that were not what he'd originally thought.

"Coffee, strong and black—the way you like it." Joel placed the mug on the table in front of him. Wyatt leaned in and breathed in the fragrance.

"It smells far better than what I make at home." He took a sip, then leaned back in his seat. "Just what I needed."

The baker frowned. "Something wrong?"

Yes, something was wrong—he'd made a dangerous move and tilted his entire world. Beth's too. Not that he could tell Joel that. "I spilled coffee everywhere this morning. Yours is better, so all is fine now." It wasn't a lie and was totally the truth.

Joel nodded, then went behind the counter. Wyatt heard the clatter of plates, then watched as the baker came back to him. "If you're not averse to muffins this hour of the day," Joel said. "These are not long out of the oven. This one is lemon," he said, pointing with a flour covered hand. "And the other is blueberry. Let me know if you require more."

"Thank you. They look and smell delicious." Wyatt lifted the lemon muffin and took a tentative bite. Joel was not wrong—it was still hot. That didn't mean he couldn't taste the wonderful flavors bursting into his mouth. He took a mouthful of coffee.

He loved the peacefulness of the bakery at this time of the day. Joel was very used to him calling in unexpectedly like this. He didn't do it daily, but it was something he did at least twice a week. The food here was excellent, and far better than anything Wyatt could make for himself. His own cooking left a lot to be desired.

He finished the first muffin and took a bite of the second. It was equally tasty in its own way. Two unique flavors, but both very appealing. Wyatt stared out onto the street. He felt very blessed to live in this small town. In the past, he'd lived in far bigger places, which also meant far more criminal activity. He liked it here, and would likely stay until he retired. Unless he was forced to leave.

He couldn't see that happening any time soon.

Joel leaned in and placed a pastry in front of him. "Try this. It's an experiment."

Wyatt picked up the strange-looking pastry and took a bite. There was an immediate flavor explosion, and he certainly wasn't complaining. "What is that? It's delicious," he said, as he took another mouthful.

Joel shrugged. "It's pastry with berries inside. I don't even know what to call it." He laughed then.

"Whatever it is, customers will flock to buy it." Wyatt finished it then reached for his wallet as he stood.

Joel shook his head. "No charge for guinea pigs," he said, but Wyatt could not be seen to be taking gifts, and threw a note on the table.

"Thanks, but I'd rather pay." He was certain Joel would understand.

His belly full, it was time to work. He headed back toward the jailhouse.

Wyatt grabbed the door handle of the sheriff's office and pushed. It was stuck, so he pushed harder. He heard a scream, then the clatter of dishes.

His heart pounded. What had he done?

The door was only slightly ajar, but it was enough for him to see around to the other side. "Oh my Lord," he growled, then waited for his deputy to help. "I'm truly sorry, Beth," he said when the door was fully opened. Both men helped the diner owner into a chair. Tommy had helped her to her feet moments earlier, and she appeared dazed. Not that Wyatt blamed her. He'd pushed the door into her as he'd tried to open it.

At least he'd done it then, and not when she had a tray full of food for the prisoners.

She closed her eyes momentarily, then glanced at him. "I'm fine," she said and began to stand, but appeared unsteady.

"Fetch the doc," Wyatt instructed Tommy. "You're bleeding," he said, noticing the pool of red on her arm. It seeped down onto her skirts. The last thing he had intended was to hurt anyone. Least of all, his friend.

Beth glanced down. Her shocked expression told him she truly hadn't realized she'd been injured in the scuffle. Wyatt pulled his handkerchief from his pocket and held it against her arm. "It doesn't appear too serious. I'm sure it will stop bleeding soon." Whether or not that was true, he wasn't certain, but wanted to keep Beth calm.

Tommy hurried back through the door. Doctor Marcus Ryan was close on his heels. "Morning Beth, Sheriff," he said as he came to stand next to Beth. "Let me see," he demanded and removed the handkerchief Wyatt held there so tenderly.

He covered her injury once more. "Hold this, Wyatt. You need stitches, Beth." Wyatt heard himself gasp. He was almost in sync with Beth. It seemed they were equally shocked. "We need to go back to the surgery. I don't have my equipment here for stitches."

The three of them headed up the road to the doctor's room. "I'm truly sorry, Beth," Wyatt said. "I don't know how it even happened." He was confused. What even cut her?

"A mug smashed on the door, and bounced onto my arm. I guess it happened then," Beth told them both.

The doctor cleaned up her arm, ensuring no pieces of crockery were in the cut, then stitched her arm and bandaged it. "No using that arm for at least a week. And no arguments. It won't heal otherwise."

She shook her head sadly. "I'll have to get someone in to help. Otherwise, I'll have to close the diner until I've healed." She appeared far from happy.

"I'm sure folks can cope for one week without the diner," the doc said, then ushered them out. The waiting room was already filling up with patients.

"I'm truly sorry, Beth," Wyatt said, as they headed back to the jailhouse to collect her belongings. Those still in one piece, that was. "This is totally my fault." He wanted to say *just like last night*, but thought the better of it. They had entered the sheriff's office, and he didn't want Tommy Garrett to know about his personal business. Besides, they both had a part in last night's fiasco.

Beth glanced up at him. "Don't you go worrying about me. What the doc doesn't know won't hurt him." Beth winced as she reached for the tray she used to deliver the meals.

Wyatt wondered what would she be like after trying to work in the diner?

"I'll help you out until your arm is alright again. It was my fault, after all." Wyatt wasn't sure why he blurted the words out, but it was too late to take them back. Besides, it was the truth. He couldn't allow Beth to lose income because of his stupidity.

Tommy stared at him at first, then laughed. "This I have got to see," he said as he shook his head. "Sheriff Wyatt Holt wearing a waitress apron. Or cooking for the diner." He laughed again, and Wyatt threw him a warning glare.

He opened the door and guided Beth outside. The fresh air felt good. He would accompany her back to the diner, and then they would decide where to go from there.

Chapter Four

Beth exhaled. This was a bad idea. A ghastly idea, in fact. Working in close proximity to Wyatt was not conducive to staying friends, she was sure of it.

Wyatt stood in the diner's kitchen and glanced about. "Show me where everything is. I know I can do this."

Beth wasn't so sure. What did a small-town sheriff know about running a diner? Diddly squat, she was certain. "Can you cook?" She held her breath while she waited for an answer.

"I watched my mother cook." His lips twitched as he said the words. Even he knew the situation was problematic.

"So that's a no." She sighed again. This was going to be a disaster. "I can get someone in. I've had Martha Cooley help before. She's an excellent cook."

Wyatt frowned. "You don't think I can handle it?" He seemed...disappointed? Did that mean he was looking forward to helping? More likely, he needed to appease his guilt.

"It wasn't your fault, Wyatt. It was purely accidental."

He reached out his hands as though he was going to cradle her, but then pulled back. "I know, but I want to do whatever I can to assist."

She nodded, but would do whatever she could to discourage him. Martha was a far better option. Whether she was available was another question entirely.

"There's plenty of time, since the diner doesn't open until noon. You can fill that kettle, though. That would be a great help. Then you can find out if Martha is available to work." That would keep him busy and out of her way. For a short time, anyway.

He glanced across at the oven. "Shall I fetch more wood?"

That was a great idea. "That would be wonderful, thank you. You can fire it up too, if you don't mind. Although, I'm sure I can manage."

"Not on my watch," Wyatt told her. "Doctor's orders."

Beth knew she had a battle on her hands. If Martha wasn't available, she didn't know what she would do. The only other option she could think of was closing the diner until the doctor gave her the all clear. It wasn't that the diner wasn't doing well. Far from it. But if customers thought the diner was closed for good, she would lose all that patronage she'd built up over the years.

Her heart thudded. It really wasn't an option.

She watched as Wyatt filled the large kettle, then fired up the stove. "How do you fill this kettle alone?" he asked. "I can barely manage it."

Beth shrugged. "I have to transfer the water from a jug. Thank you for doing it," she said, then felt the need to sit down.

Wyatt rushed to her side. "Are you alright? Should I fetch the doc again?"

She almost glared at him, but controlled herself. "I don't need the doctor," she said, feeling somewhat fierce about the entire situation. Not only had she strained their relationship by kissing her best friend, her entire livelihood was thrown off kilter by an accident neither of them had control over.

Wyatt turned pained eyes to her. "I'm truly sorry," he said, and she knew it was true. Wyatt would never intentionally hurt anyone. Especially not her. "I'll fetch Martha, shall I?"

"That's a good idea," Beth said, and watched Wyatt's retreating back as he left the diner.

It seemed like forever before Wyatt arrived back at the diner with Martha, but in reality it was less than half an hour. In the meantime, Beth had written out today's menu for Martha and checked her supplies.

She would send Wyatt to the mercantile to top those up, provided Martha could help. Otherwise, it would negate all her plans. She would *not* allow Wyatt to run her kitchen while she recovered. His heart was in the right place, but he had to face facts—he was no cook.

It would hurt his feelings, but better that than having him harm her business. Beth was certain he would understand. She might not be the richest business in town, but she had a steady clientele. There wasn't a day when the diner wasn't at least partially full, and if she was honest with herself, those were her most favorite times.

Apart from the fact it was less hectic, she had the time to sit and talk with her customers. They seemed to enjoy it too. The thing Beth enjoyed the most about running the diner was spending time with people.

Most of her day was spent in the kitchen preparing for meals. She visited the mercantile for supplies, but mostly she ordered well in advance. It was only when she ran short that Beth went there in between orders. Items that required special storage, such as milk, cream, and butter, were different. She bought them as required.

"I'm sorry about your injury," Martha said, pulling on a linen apron. She took the handwritten menu Beth handed her and studied it. "I can stay as long as you need it. A week, two weeks, or even longer. Whatever you need."

Beth was elated. Forgetting about her condition, she clapped her hands, but instantly regretted it. She winced in pain and instead placed her hands in her lap. "You'll never know how much I appreciate it," she told the other woman. "The accident has certainly upset everything." She glanced across at Wyatt, worried her words would make him feel guilty all over again. He studied her, and Beth knew her words had cut him to the core. "It's not your fault, Wyatt," she reiterated.

He nodded, but didn't appear to be appeased. "What can I do to help?"

If helping eased his guilt, then she would let him help in whatever way he could. "Maybe set the tables? I can tell you what to do." She raised her eyebrows at him. That might seem like women's work, but he'd done all the heavy work to date. "Later, I'll get you to go to the mercantile and bring back supplies. I'll even feed you." She laughed then. Wyatt loved good food, and they both knew it.

"I need to start the soup and bread now. Wyatt, here is the list of supplies. Can you go to the mercantile right away and have this list fulfilled? That would be a big help." Martha was good at getting people to do what was required, and right now, it made Beth happy. If the soup wasn't started soon, it wouldn't be ready in time.

Wyatt took the list. "Of course," he said, then hurried out the door.

"Martha, you are a godsend," Beth told her. "Wyatt wanted to run the diner for me."

Martha grimaced. "His heart is in the right place, I'm sure, but can you imagine?" Both women laughed. It felt good to laugh, but the movement sent pain shooting down her arm, and Beth flinched.

"You really are in pain, aren't you? Here," Martha said as she grabbed a chair. "You sit down and rest. I'll make you a nice cup of tea. In fact, you should go home. I have everything in hand."

Martha was right. Beth knew she was, but for today, she didn't want to leave. She'd make sure everything was running smoothly before she would feel comfortable doing that. It wasn't like this was the first time Martha had taken over for her. She'd done it several times before. Especially after Beth's husband had died—her friend had been a tower of strength. Without her, Beth may not have got through the most difficult time of her life.

"What can I do?" Beth asked, already knowing the answer.

"Not a thing. Make yourself comfortable. I really wish you would go home, Beth. I'm sure Wyatt would walk you home."

The man in question walked into the kitchen at that very moment. "Of course I will." He placed the box of supplies on the kitchen counter. "Where do you want these?"

Martha glanced in the box. "I'll use most of them soon, so there is fine. Please take Beth home. She's in pain, and I'm perfectly fine here."

"Consider it done." Wyatt reached out a hand to Beth, and she took it. She wasn't sure why she did, but Wyatt's expression was one of worry, and she didn't want him to worry about her. It was bad enough he blamed himself for the accident. And it was simply that—an accident. If she'd still been handing out food to the prisoners, or he had arrived moments later, it would not have happened. But that's what accidents were—totally unavoidable incidents that no one could predict.

Wyatt helped Beth to her feet. She felt a little unsteady, but knowing Wyatt was by her side helped. "Are you alright?" he asked. How did he know? The man could see right through her.

"A little lightheaded," she answered. "Give me a moment. I'll be fine." She clutched his arm and stood for a moment until the dizziness passed. He stared down at her, concern etch in his face.

"I think we should go back to the doc," Wyatt said, clearly concerned.

Beth shook her head, and the dizziness returned. She sat down for a few minutes. This was frustrating. Each time it happened, it seemed to convince Wyatt she clearly wasn't fine. He was mothering her, and it didn't sit right with Beth.

"Why don't I get you that cup of tea," Martha said. "Tea is good in any situation." She didn't wait for an answer, and instead filled a mug with tea. "Coffee for you, Sheriff?" Again, she didn't wait for an answer. "Why don't you take Beth and sit her at one of the tables?"

Beth was happy about the interruption. Hopefully, it would take Wyatt's mind off having her checked over by the doctor again.

He helped her to her feet again, and this time, Beth felt better. Perhaps she'd stood too quickly? Wyatt gripped her tightly. She felt secure with his arm around her back, and could do this all day. If only she wasn't injured and in pain.

Chapter Five

Wyatt studied Beth as she sat opposite. She had always been a strong woman. At least in the time he knew her.

Now, thanks to him, she was reduced to being reliant on everyone else. He closed his eyes momentarily and the vision of a broken mug covered in blood, her blood, returned. There was little he could do to help, but he would do whatever it took.

The first thing he would do was see her settled. Then he would visit with Tommy and let him know he was taking the next week off, so his deputy would be in charge. Wyatt would be around, so if anything dire came up, he would help. Nothing like that had occurred in the time he'd lived in Crystal Springs, and it was not something he expected to happen.

"Eat up while it's hot," Martha said, placing breakfast in front of them both.

Wyatt glanced down. Bacon, eggs, sausages, and toast on the side. Beth had oats, her preferred early morning meal. "I've already eaten," Wyatt said, but Martha waved his words aside.

"Since when did Wyatt Holt refuse food?" Both women laughed, and he shrugged. A lot had happened since he'd been at the diner.

Beth reached out for the jug of milk. "Let me do that," Wyatt said, reaching across the table to secure the jug. She glanced up and smiled at him, and nodded. His heart fluttered, but he had no idea why.

"Thank you," Beth said. "That's plenty."

They said a prayer of thanks for their food, then tucked in. Wyatt often skipped breakfast. It was simply another thing he had to do. He had coffee and occasionally visited the bakery. Joel made the best pastries and muffins he'd ever eaten. And he'd had plenty over his forty-plus years. That was one good thing about being an early riser—the bakery goods were still warm when he arrived.

"Martha is an excellent cook," he said between mouthfuls.

"That she is," Beth answered, then went back to her oats before speaking again. "Wyatt," she said slowly. "I don't want you to feel guilty about any of this. Nor do I want you feeling obligated to help. It's all under control."

He placed his knife and fork on the side of his place. "This *is* my fault," he said firmly. "I don't feel obligated, but want to help a friend. Or am I being pushy?"

She frowned, and his heart pounded. The last thing Wyatt wanted was to push Beth away. If she thought he was being forceful, it might harm their friendship. The kiss they'd shared had already done its share of damage.

"Not pushy, but maybe a little more assertive than normal?" She sighed then. "Wyatt, I can manage. I have Martha to help, and the diner will run smoothly as though nothing is amiss."

"I'm taking the week off," he blurted out, and watched as her frown turned to a grimace.

"That's just stupid," she said gruffly, then ate more of her oats.

Wyatt was shocked at her words, but didn't respond. He went back to his food, and they didn't speak for the rest of the meal.

Wyatt carried their soiled dishes into the kitchen. It was the least he could do. "Can I walk you home?" he asked Beth. "Then I'll check in with Tommy, and let him know he's on his own for the week."

"Honestly, Wyatt," Beth said, exasperation clear in her tone. "Martha and I can cope."

"I know," he said, shrugging his shoulders as he spoke. "I need to feel like I'm doing something. Anything."

Beth raised her eyebrows. "I guess there are things you can do to help. Like chopping the wood for the fire, carrying groceries, and doing other errands." He could hear in her voice she was merely humoring him, but Wyatt didn't care. At least he wouldn't feel so bad.

She stood as he turned to leave. "Wyatt," she said, stepping toward him. "Thank you for your help." Beth then stretched up and kissed his cheek. It took all his effort not to touch the place her lips had been.

"Nothing to thank me for," he said, then hurried outside before things became even more personal. He might long to kiss Beth the way she'd kissed him the night before, but he refused to give in to his feelings. Especially given the circumstances she now found herself in. The problem was, how long could he keep up the pretence?

That kiss changed everything.

"What do you mean, you're taking a week off? Because of Beth's injury?" Tommy shook his head. "That don't make sense."

Wyatt frowned. "Sure it does." He slid down into the sheriff's chair. His chair. He felt comfortable there. It was like being home. Except his cottage wasn't like home – it was more an empty shell. There was something missing there, and he knew what it was. Or should he say *who* it was? "It's my fault Beth is incapacitated, so I'm making amends."

Tommy opened his mouth to speak, but Wyatt interrupted him. "Don't even say it," he said, glaring at his deputy. "You must have something to do, instead of throwing accusations about." Not that Tommy had spoken. Wyatt hadn't given him the chance.

"All I was going to say was…" he chuckled then. "I can only imagine you in that cute apron Beth wears at the diner." This time, he laughed.

Wyatt knew he shouldn't be annoyed, but he was. "I'm not cooking, smarty pants. Martha Cooley is helping in that regard. I'm just doing all the heavy stuff—like chopping wood and carting groceries."

"And eating the excellent food," Tommy added, then put his hands up in defence.

Wyatt shoved his chair back and snatched up his hat. "That's it, I'm off." He strode to the door, then turned to face his deputy. "Let me know if there are any problems." He slammed the door behind him.

He was like a bear with a sore head, and Wyatt knew it. Not sleeping last night wasn't helping. It wasn't like he couldn't go a night without decent shut-eye, because he'd gone days at a time when needed, but this was different. His mind was constantly spinning and running through all the scenarios. Plus, he was reliving that kiss.

Wyatt groaned. Why did Beth have to kiss him? The question really was, why did he give into his feelings? After two years of keeping his distance, suddenly he couldn't. He didn't know if it was the moonlight, the semi-darkness, or simply the fact Beth was right there with him amid all that.

She had been his friend almost from the moment he arrived. One of his first places to visit was the diner. The food had been excellent, still was, and he visited often. She'd sat down with him a few times, when it wasn't busy, and chatted. She asked about his previous placements and told him she was a widow. She also said she didn't have children. Apart from that, he didn't know a great deal about her.

What he knew was he like her. A lot. And going by her actions the previous night, she liked him too.

Wyatt groaned again. He loved it here in Crystal Springs. He didn't want to leave and certainly didn't want to lose Beth's friendship. Between the kiss and him hitting her with the door, everything had become a nightmare in less than twelve hours.

What he did about it was the question.

Right now, he didn't know the answer to that, but he was on leave, and not currently the sheriff. For a change, he would be Wyatt Holt, the person. It was time to change out of his sheriff's uniform. Or at the very least, take off his badge.

Chapter Six

"You know he's sweet on you," Martha said after Wyatt had left. Beth stared at her. How could Martha even know that? "It's clear you're interested in him, too."

That made Beth blush. She felt heat creep up her neck and into her cheeks. "You've got it all wrong," she said firmly, despite knowing her face had to be bright red. "Wyatt is a friend."

Martha laughed as she kneaded the bread. "If you say so," she said, raising her eyebrows. "You're like a pair of love-sick teenagers. I have no idea why you don't just marry him."

Beth sputtered. "What? Get…" She shook her head. "We're not even courting! Not that we plan to." Her head was spinning. Where had this even come from?

"Why not?" Martha asked as she put the bread dough aside to rise. She turned to the stove and gave the soup a stir. "You've been falling over each other for the past two years. Everyone in town knows you're sweet on each other. Dennis at the mercantile made sure of that."

"Dennis?" Beth was incredulous. "Since when did Dennis become a matchmaker?" She laughed then, as though it was a joke. However, if Dennis was spreading rumors about her and Wyatt, it was no laughing matter.

Beth slunk down into a chair. She wanted to put her head in her hands and cry, but that would do nothing to stop the gossips. And there were several of those around Crystal Springs.

"You don't spend much time at the mercantile, do you?" Martha asked as she laughed. "Dennis loves to match up the townsfolk."

Beth shook her head. She was incredulous about this new information. "I'm in and out of there as quickly as I can. Mostly I leave a list and leave."

"That will be the reason," Martha said. "He tried to match me up with Joel once, but we were having none of it."

"You don't like Joel?"

Martha licked her lips. "On the contrary. We do like each other. We've been friends for years. The fact Dennis tried to match us, put both of us off spending time together." She sighed then. Did that mean Martha liked Joel more than she was letting on? "After I became a widow, I've mostly kept to myself. I couldn't bear another heartache like I did when I lost my husband."

Beth wanted to take Martha in her arms and hug her. She refrained because not only would her arm hurt like the dickens, but she was certain both of them would end up in tears. Becoming a widow was the last thing either of them expected at such a young age.

Martha wiped at her eyes, and Beth knew she was right to hold back. Suddenly she straightened her back and stared toward Beth. "Do you think Wyatt will return for lunch?"

Beth hoped he would, but wouldn't count on it. "Not intentionally, knowing Wyatt. He's stubborn, that one."

Speak of the devil, the door opened a short time later, and Wyatt strolled inside. "Afternoon, ladies," he said, heading toward the kitchen. "What can I do for you?" He rubbed his hands together as if in glee. To Beth, there was little to be happy about right now.

"Coffee?" Martha asked, but didn't wait for an answer. She handed the mug to Wyatt and ushered him into a chair.

"I didn't come for coffee," he said, frustration clear in his voice. "but I'd never refuse a good coffee. I came to help. What do you need?"

"Right now? For you to sit down and drink your coffee. I'll join you for a tea. I have time." Beth rolled her eyes, then sat on the opposite side of the table, despite Wyatt still standing. "For goodness' sake, Wyatt. Sit down. Having you tower over me is very…disconcerting." He sat down, but didn't seem happy about it.

"Early lunch," Martha said, placing a bowl of thick vegetable soup in front of them both. It wasn't long before she returned with a plate of bread and a lump of butter.

Wyatt looked down at the food and leaned forward, breathing in the aroma. "Smells delicious, but I didn't come here to eat," he said gruffly.

"Oh, for goodness' sake, Wyatt. Just eat it. We'll find plenty for you to do later, if that's what you really want." Beth was feeling cantankerous. She wasn't sure if it was the pain she was in, or the fact Wyatt kept refusing food. The man had to eat, after all.

"Yes, Ma'am," he said with a grin, and giving a brief salute.

Martha joined them, and they said grace. It wouldn't be long before the diner opened for lunch, and it would be hectic. This was probably the only time all three of them would get to sit down and eat in peace.

"I'll need you to help deliver meals to the tables," Martha told him. "Will that work for you?"

Wyatt studied her momentarily. "Show me what to do, and I will do it. I'm a fast learner," he told her. As she watched him, Beth decided he appeared uncomfortable. Was it the thought of delivering meals to customers, or something else entirely? It made her wonder what he would have been like if she'd taken up his offer to cook. She couldn't even imagine him in her tiny kitchen—the man was a giant—his head almost hit the doorframe when he entered a room.

Looking him over, Beth knew something was different about Wyatt, but couldn't put her finger on it. Martha must have noticed it too, since she appeared to be studying him as they ate.

"Where's your sheriff's badge?" Martha's words held shock, and Beth realized that's what it was. His usually shiny badge was missing. In fact, he wasn't in the usual outfit he wore each day.

"It's at home. Tommy is taking over for the week." He leaned back in his chair and glanced at the two women. "I haven't had time off since I arrived here two years ago. I'm entitled to a break."

Beth felt like rolling her eyes. "Except it's not a break. You keep insinuating yourself into working here at the diner." Oh, she knew what he was thinking. It wasn't work, he was helping a friend.

She knew he was right, but guilt should not be a reason for him to take a week off work. "I appreciate it, Wyatt, but you truly didn't have to…"

His head shot around to face her. "I totally did. I did this to you, and this is my recompense. Let me do this for you, Beth."

His eyes pleaded with her, and for the very first time, she saw the little boy in him. It was as though his life depended on her answer. How could she refuse him when he asked this way?

She nodded briskly. "Alright. We'll find plenty for you to do. I hear you're handy with a hammer? I have lots of things that need fixing around the place."

Wyatt frowned. "Why didn't you ask before?"

Beth bit her bottom lip. "I don't know," she finally answered.

"I do," Martha interjected. "She's a stubborn so and so. Much like you." Her eyes danced with mischief, and it made them all laugh.

Soon lunch was over, and a few customers rolled into the diner.

Chapter Seven

Wyatt could get very used to this. Cooked meals at least twice a day was appealing. Joel's pastries were good, but Martha's cooking was better. Beth's better still.

The trouble was, if this kept up, he could see himself putting on weight. Especially since he wouldn't be doing rounds each day. Perhaps he could offer to do that for Tommy—to help him out.

Almost the moment the thought hit, he discounted it. He'd made a commitment to Beth, and he would stick with it. Besides, it wasn't as though he didn't want to help his friend. That was the whole reason he'd taken the week off.

He could tell she was in pain, despite Beth denying it. He noticed every time she winced, and he felt her pain. It cut right through him.

Wyatt shook himself mentally. Beth would be furious if she knew he still blamed himself for what happened to her. She had refuted his claim several times now, and at first it had annoyed him. Probably because he believed he was culpable for Beth's injuries. It wasn't like she was merely bruised. The inside of her dominant arm was seriously cut from a little above her wrist, for about four inches. His quick thinking of putting pressure on it to stop the bleeding had been imperative, according to Doc Ryan.

Now he wondered if she truly needed to go back. At the very least, Wyatt thought some sort of painkiller was in order. Laudanum would probably do the trick, but that was the doc's area of expertise.

Besides, getting Beth to agree to have her stitches checked in the next day or two was probably non-existent.

He stood and carried the dishes to the kitchen. "I can do that," Martha called to his back.

Wyatt called back. "Too late, I have them." Then he checked the wood box. It was getting low. The oven had been working since early this morning, and it was apparent the diner went through a power of wood. The two women joined him in the kitchen. "I'm going out to cut more wood," he said, then left before anyone had a chance to answer.

In the small yard behind the diner, he reached for a block of wood. These pieces were huge, and it made him wonder how Beth managed. Surely she didn't cut this herself? It was then he remembered she'd told him a while back one of the young men from town cut it for a handful of dollars each week. He searched his brain for the young man's name. Wyatt would pay him a visit and give him whatever money he'd lost. This exercise was not about robbing a young man of extra money—it was about helping Beth and easing his mind.

While he may be used to chopping wood for his own use, Wyatt was far from prepared for the hard work of cutting enough to run the diner's oven. Today had been an eye-opener, and he wondered how its owner managed alone. From what he understood, Beth and her husband had run the diner together. It must have been a difficult transition for her.

At least with Martha living in town, she had back-up when required. He stood back and admired his handiwork, glad for the foresight of changing into old clothes. Beth had a small shed where the wood was piled up, ready to go inside as needed.

Wyatt ran a sleeved arm across his forehead. This was seriously hard work. Perhaps not for a younger man, but someone of his age, especially when he wasn't used to it. His muscles were already complaining. Wyatt was certain tonight would be worse.

He opened the back door and went inside. "Where's your toolbox?" he asked. "I can start on those jobs you need doing."

Beth stared at him with sad eyes. "Why don't we just rest for a bit?" she asked, then pointed at a nearby table. "You look plum tuckered out."

He grunted. "I'm not used to cutting wood. Don't worry, I'll do more tomorrow. I won't leave you short."

"No, you won't," Beth said firmly. "Jonathan Hornsby will be here tomorrow, and he will cut the rest. He won't be happy you've done some of his work."

She was probably right. "I'd intended to cover whatever he lost. I don't want you to run out."

"Wyatt Holt!" she said, putting her good hand to her hip. "This diner has run perfectly well without you for many years, and will continue to do so. If you want to hang around, that's fine, but I can't have you interfering with my well oiled system."

Wyatt stared at her. He was shocked more than anything, since he'd never seen Beth behave in this way. But he had already admitted he didn't know her as well as he would like to. He stood silently for a minute, taking it all in. Then he shuffled his feet and braced himself. "I apologize," he said quietly. "I was only trying to help."

He turned and walked away. He'd made her mad, and that was not Wyatt's intention. He planned to do the exact opposite. What he would do now, he didn't know. This was supposed to be about making amends for his stupidity. It wasn't supposed to cause a rift between them, but that's exactly what happened.

As he opened the door, Beth's hand on his arm caused him to stop. He stared down into her anguish filled face. "No, I'm sorry. I guess I'm frustrated about this entire situation. Please stay." Tears danced in her eyes, and he wanted to kiss her distress away. Instead, he pulled her close, being careful not to touch her injured arm.

"This is all new to me," Wyatt said gently. "I want to help, but guess I went too far."

Beth tipped her head to stare into his face. "You did. I'm happy to have you around, but you can't overstep." She smiled tentatively then. "If you're still willing, I have some minor jobs that need doing."

His heart fluttered. A simple smile could send his heart a flutter? When had things changed between them? Of course, Wyatt knew the answer—it was Beth's kiss. Why had she done that? Things would never be the same between them. That was the pity of it all.

"Wyatt?" Her voice brought him back to the present. "What are you thinking?" She glanced at him curiously.

Instead of answering, he leaned in and kissed her lips, then suddenly pulled back. "I shouldn't have done that," he said, and wanted to retreat. Perhaps for the next twenty years.

Laughter danced in Beth's eyes. "Why not? It was nice."

He wanted to kiss her again and again.

Now he knew he was really in trouble. Never in his entire life had Wyatt wanted to be with a woman more. He'd had flings over the years, but that was it. Nothing special—not like this. He could see himself with Beth for the rest of their lives, and that was not a good thing.

Not given his profession and the risks involved. Although if he stayed here in Crystal Springs where it was peaceful and virtually crime-free, things might be different. If he was transferred elsewhere, that could be a whole different scenario.

Beth stared at him, waiting for an answer. As much as he wanted to kiss her again, hold her close, and never let go, it wasn't the right thing to do. "We can't do this," he said gruffly, then left the diner.

Chapter Eight

Beth stared after Wyatt's retreating back. What just happened?

Perhaps she'd gone overboard when she told him to stop. Or maybe he was scared? But scared of what? Of her, or of what might happen between them? Was it the fact she was a widow, and he'd never been married?

She truly didn't know, and wasn't sure what she should do to remedy the situation. Beth spun around and went back to the kitchen, where Martha was busy washing dishes. With the lunch break over, all was quiet again, thank goodness. She didn't want anyone to witness their brief exchange.

Martha turned to face her. "What's wrong?" she asked the moment Beth came into view. "Had your first disagreement?" She laughed then, and Beth knew she thought it was a joke.

"Something like that." Beth closed her eyes and felt tears roll down her face. She wasn't a crier, never had been, but she was devastated. She had pined after Wyatt almost since the moment he arrived in town. She really liked him, and he liked her. Unfortunately for Beth, it seemed things had gone beyond *like* now. Whether it was merely familiarity, she wasn't sure. Her fondness for Wyatt had grown over time to the point she wanted to kiss him. To hold him and be with him.

Had she driven him away with that small action? That brief kiss? Hot tears fell and she couldn't stop them.

"Oh, Beth," Martha said gently. "What happened? It's not like Wyatt to be cruel."

"Not cruel, just truthful." She hiccupped on a sob, and Martha pulled her closer. "I did a terrible thing last night," she told her friend between sobs.

Martha pushed her gently away and stared into her face. "What did you do?"

Beth could see the concern on her face. "I kissed him," she said, then shook her head. "I shouldn't have done that." It took all her control not to cry again. Beth felt as though her world had ended. With that one small action, she had driven away her best friend.

"Good on you," Martha said, surprising Beth. "It's about time you acted on your feelings."

"He didn't kiss me back. Not then, anyway. Until today." Beth wiped a stray tear from her face.

"I don't see what the problem is." She seemed perplexed, and Beth suddenly understood why.

"He ended by saying *we can't do this*, then left." Her heart pounded, and she was developing a headache. No doubt the amount of crying she'd done had caused that. She couldn't bear to think how blotchy and red her face must be. There was no way Beth was going out in public until her face cleared.

"The jug has boiled. I'll make tea," Martha said firmly. "There's some lemon cake left from lunch as well." She ushered Beth into a chair, then went to pour the tea. When she returned, Martha stared at her until Beth felt uncomfortable. "Neither of us are young," she finally said. "Wyatt included. You've been married, he hasn't." She reached across the table and held Beth's hand. "I think he's afraid."

Martha's words startled her. Wyatt afraid? Not likely. The man had gone up against murderers and criminals of all levels. He'd killed men in self-defence, been shot multiple times, and arrested some of the worst criminals of all time, forcing them into jail. It was all Beth could do not to laugh. "Wyatt isn't afraid of anything."

Martha squeezed her hand. "Most men are afraid of love. Just because Wyatt is a tough lawman does not mean he knows what to do when it comes to women."

Just when Beth thought she couldn't be shocked any more, Martha's words rang true to her. Could that be the problem with Wyatt? Was he afraid to love her? She stared at Martha, afraid to open her mouth in case she cried again.

"You know I'm right," Martha said. "Now drink your tea and eat some cake. If Wyatt were here, that cake would be demolished in no time."

Her words made Beth laugh. She knew it was true. Sitting there at the table without Wyatt suddenly felt wrong. "I miss him already," Beth whispered.

"Of course you do," Martha said gently. "We'll find a way to coax him back."

Beth hoped her friend was right.

Beth busied herself as much as possible, given her situation. She saw Wyatt through the dining room window, wandering aimlessly up and down the boardwalk. It made her wonder if he was debating coming back and had rethought their predicament. Well, his really—Beth had no doubts about what they should do.

She guessed Wyatt might be worried about how the townsfolk would see things, but she didn't care. What business was it of anyone else's who Wyatt courted? It had absolutely nothing to do with them, and he needed to understand that.

She stared out the window for longer than she knew she should. If Martha hadn't interrupted her, she would still be there. "Still pounding the boardwalk, is he? That's a good sign," she said, putting a hand on Beth's shoulder. "It means he's having second thoughts."

Beth wasn't so sure. He'd taken the week off. What else was he going to do with his time? Suddenly, Wyatt turned and stared at the diner. Did he see her watching him? In a matter of seconds, he headed toward them.

"Quick, into the kitchen," Beth said. She didn't want Wyatt to think she cared, even though she did. She would not pressure him to do something he didn't want to do. And that included loving her.

They had only just made it into the kitchen when the front door opened. Martha turned and acted surprised when he entered the room. "Oh, Wyatt, I thought you'd gone." She glared at him, as only Martha could do.

"Well, I'm back. What are the jobs you want done?" Beth could see he was remorseful, but that meant nothing unless he changed his mind. Not that she would force him into anything. She only wished they could go back to the way things were.

If she was honest with herself, that wasn't true. She wanted to move forward and see if they could make anything of an actual relationship. If it didn't work out, then it could be a problem. Crystal Springs was not big, far from it. So they would still have to deal with each other on a daily basis.

That thought cut her to the core.

"There are screws loose on some of the cupboard doors, and shelves that are loose. Lots of little things that need fixing," Martha said, then handed him the small toolbox Beth's husband had stored in a corner cupboard.

Seeing it brought back memories, and she suddenly felt guilty about pursuing Wyatt. She spun around and ran out of the diner, taking in the fresh air outside. Beth sat on the wooden bench close to the diner, simply contemplating her life as it was now. Perhaps this was not a good time to think about another relationship.

She knew she was being silly. Or more likely, sensitive. It had been many years since she'd seen that toolbox, and it had hit her hard.

"I'm sorry, Joe," she whispered. "We both know I must get on with my life." It had been a long time since Beth had talked to her dead husband. Probably too long, but she had decided to move on with her life. Never had she believed she would become a widow at thirty, but a runaway horse and wagon saw to that. The memory of it all tore at her heart all over again.

"Beth?" Wyatt's voice cut through her thoughts. "Are you alright?" She glanced up, and he shook his head. "Clearly you're not." He came to sit down next to her. "I can fetch my own toolbox if that helps. Martha told me it was your late husband's." He looked concerned for her.

"I guess it was a shock, that's all. I haven't seen the toolbox for nearly a decade." She swallowed hard then. Why did memories from so long ago affect her like this? She was startled when Wyatt reached for her hand and squeezed it.

"I'm sure my conduct this morning didn't help. I'm truly sorry."

He sounded genuine and appeared remorseful. Unfortunately, that didn't change things. "Apology accepted," Beth said warily. Where did that leave them? "We should go back to only being friends."

Her words seemed to shock him, and Wyatt suddenly let go of her hand. "Is that what you really want?" he asked, concern in his voice. "I know I was hasty in my decision."

Now she was in a quandary. Should they pick up where they left off, or go back as Wyatt seemed to suggest? She honestly didn't know what was best— for either of them. That meant she wasn't sure how to answer. Instead, she studied him.

He picked up her hand again and kissed it. "This is all my fault," he told her. "Everything that's happened, the kiss, the injury, and the breakup—it's all on me." He shook his head sadly. "You are far better off without me. That's what I tried to say earlier, but messed it up."

Beth turned to face him. "I regret nothing," she whispered, then leaned in and kissed him again. Wyatt's hands came up and cupped her face, and the kiss deepened. What would people think? They were in plain sight in the middle of town. She opened her eyes momentarily to see if anyone was around.

No one was there except the two of them, so she closed her eyes again and enjoyed the moment.

Chapter Nine

Wyatt was more confused than ever. Beth was hot, then she was cold. To be fair, he wasn't much different himself. At their age, making a commitment to another person was difficult. For Beth, it was harder still. She likely still felt loyalty to her dead husband, and that surely had her pulling in all directions.

He didn't blame her. Not that he'd ever been married, but he almost was once. Then he came to his senses. He could tell her heart wasn't in it. As it turned out, it was probably the best thing he could have done. Less than six months after they broke up, his fiancée married someone else. A rich rancher. Someone who could give her a far better life than Wyatt ever could.

Perhaps that's what was best for Beth. Someone with loads of money. He'd saved most of his earnings—what was a sheriff stuck in the middle of nowhere going to spend his money on, after all? Once he retired, he could build a house and make a new life for himself. At worst, he would be killed before he did anything useful with it.

"Wyatt," Beth's sweet voice interrupted his thoughts. "What are you worried about? People talking?"

He wasn't sure and should be honest. "I don't know. It's a big step. I mean…"

She put her fingers to his lips to stop him from talking. "Bigger for me, but I have to move forward. I like you, and you like me. At least I think you do. What else is there to worry about?"

Wyatt frowned. "Of course I like you. Why else would I let you kiss me?" He chuckled then, and it felt good. Since the kiss last night, he'd felt irritated. His entire world had tilted, his beliefs had all been turned around.

A slow smile crossed Beth's lips, and warmth flooded him. "Sheriffs have a reputation, you know." She threw him a coy look then, and shivers went down his spine. She might have been playing with him, but it set his heart to racing. If this continued, things might get out of control.

Instead, he stood and helped Beth to her feet. "I need to get to work on those chores you set. I'll accompany you back inside, then get my toolbox." It was obvious the sight of Joe's toolbox upset Beth more than she was willing to admit, and he would not allow that to continue.

He held her hand and led Beth inside. "Thank you," she whispered. When he left her, she was talking with Martha.

On his stroll back home, Wyatt encountered a few of the townsfolk. "Morning, Sheriff," one person said.

"Morning," he answered, not correcting them. Officially, he was still sheriff, but this week, he was not doing sheriff duties. He was being a regular person. Whatever that was. Wyatt had his first appointment as sheriff at the ripe old age of twenty-four. It was his hometown, and they were desperate. His place of employment, the mercantile, had burned down, and he was out of work. The previous sheriff had a heart attack and there was no one else to take the job.

Little did Wyatt know the heartache and the loneliness he would endure over the next twenty or so years of doing his job. He wasn't sure he was ready to fall in love—with anyone. Yet here he was contemplating a life with Beth Hughes, the woman who grabbed his attention on the very day they met.

As he unlocked the door to his cottage, Wyatt wondered exactly what he was doing. Walking through the small building, he realized this was not a place to bring a wife. It was designed for one person, and one person only—the sheriff. No town expected their sheriff to marry. It was an unwritten rule. Life as a lawman was dangerous. Some lived to an old age, but many didn't.

Beth had already lost one husband. Did he really want to put her in a position where she might lose another? He shook his head sadly. It certainly wasn't his plan, but Wyatt didn't know how to do anything else. Besides, he enjoyed being a lawman. And he was good at what he did.

"Hello?" Tommy's voice rang through the cottage.

That was all he needed—an inquisition. "In here, Tommy," Wyatt called back from the kitchen. He heard the shuffle of feet, and then his deputy stood in the doorway, scrutinizing him.

"I wasn't sure it was you. I saw the open door." He nodded to the open cupboard. "What are you up to? I thought you were helping Beth?"

Did he think Wyatt was just lounging about? Well, he'd be wrong. "Getting my toolbox. Beth needs cupboard doors and shelves fixed." Finally, he found what he was looking for and pulled it from the very back.

"She hasn't got one?" Tommy stared at him curiously.

Wyatt felt like rolling his eyes. Why was the deputy always so curious? Then he realized it came with the job. "She only has the one her husband used."

"Oh," Tommy said, then shrugged his shoulders. Wyatt guessed he understood. "Guess they're feeding you well over there?"

"They are," Wyatt said tersely. Did Tommy think he was only doing this for the food? "If you'll excuse me…" He stood and shoved past the other man. "Lock the door as you leave," he said, then hurried back to the diner.

The aroma of the roast cooking in the oven was enticing. He'd been loaded up with coffee and cake throughout the afternoon, to the point he was bursting at the seams. But that didn't stop him from almost drooling at the smells permeating the kitchen.

As he repaired each cupboard, he watched Martha as she prepared the evening's meals. He could certainly see himself doing this each day. He knew it would never happen. He was a sheriff, not a handyman. Besides, once the week was over, he'd be back to his sheriff duties.

"Wyatt," Beth said, her hand resting on his shoulder. "I really appreciate your help. It's a pity you don't do this as a regular job."

He turned to face her and wasn't sure what she was thinking. Did she mean because she would see him more? Or it would mean he would no longer be the sheriff? Beth was often hard to read. "I wouldn't say no to that. This kitchen fills my senses with delicious smells." He chuckled then and returned the tools to their rightful place. "What else needs fixing?" He glanced around the room, trying to pull his attention away from her hand on his shoulder. Knowing she was so close sent all sorts of feelings through him. Fight them as he would, they seemed to get stronger instead of going away as he'd hoped.

"Since you've been so helpful," Martha told him, "you'll get to taste what you long to eat." She laughed, and Beth joined her. Warmth flooded him and Wyatt couldn't help but join in. Maybe it wasn't such a bad idea spending time here. The rewards were far greater than any monetary reward he received from being the town sheriff.

He shook himself mentally. What he really needed to do was spend less time here, not more. Every time he found himself in Beth's company, his feelings for her grew stronger. Not that he didn't already like her, but now he longed to be with her all the time.

Once again, it was his fault. He was the one who decided to take a week from work to look after her. Not that Beth needed that. She could clearly fend for herself. That was a good thing. He liked an independent woman. Someone who could make decisions for herself, and could run her business her own way.

Several years ago, he might not have thought that way. Back then, he was a fool. He didn't see women the way he did now. He believed they were meant to be wives and nothing else. Moving from town to town with his job meant he witnessed women running their own businesses, shunning marriage for their own place in the world. He also saw how poorly some of those women were treated, and he didn't like it one iota. Wherever possible, he stepped in to help ease the prejudice against women, but he was only one person.

"What else needs fixing?" Wyatt picked up his toolbox, inferior as it was to Joe's, and glanced about. "Didn't you say there was a loose shelf?"

"This one," Beth said, pointing to a shelf near the door. "We don't put a lot of weight on it, because it's so fragile." She reached out to touch it at the same time Wyatt did, and their hands touched. She pulled her hand away quickly.

Wyatt glanced down at her as he continued to wiggle the shelf. "I can fix that, but it seems high for both of you ladies."

"It was perfect for Joe," Beth whispered.

He wiggled it again. Perhaps he could change that. "I can lower it and make it easier for you two. How does that sound?"

Beth's face lit up. "That would be wonderful. Thank you," she said, then stepped forward and hugged him with one arm. He knew he shouldn't, but Wyatt revelled in her closeness. He put the tools aside and wrapped his arms around her. She felt so fragile, so vulnerable, and he wanted to do all he could to protect her.

He was certain that wasn't the sheriff in him coming to the surface, but the man. The one who was quickly falling in love with his best friend.

Chapter Ten

Beth pulled herself out of Wyatt's embrace. She'd done it again. She had let herself get carried away with him. The only thing Beth could put it down to was her situation. Right now, she felt more defenceless than she had for a long time. If she was truthful, since Joe had been killed.

It felt as though she was grieving all over again, which didn't make sense. She'd gone all these years and coped. When she thought back, two things had changed—she'd kissed the sheriff, and Joe's toolbox had resurfaced.

Her injury didn't seem to come into play, except for the fact she'd seen more of Wyatt in the past day than she had all week. Being so close to him, spending so much time with him, it was not good for her peace of mind.

She was a widow, for goodness' sake. She wasn't meant to pine after a man who wasn't her husband. Except she had feelings for Wyatt, and didn't know what to do about it.

The rattle of dishes in the background reminded her they were not alone.

"We'll have extra customers tonight," Beth suddenly told Martha. "Did I tell you that?"

Martha turned to her, eyes penetrating. It was a distraction, and they both knew it. "No, you didn't. What do you want me to do? Anything special in mind?"

"There will be plenty of roast, but maybe add another dessert to the menu? Apple pie is reasonably quick to put together."

"Sounds good. I already have a cherry cobbler prepared, so that will be an excellent alternative." Martha turned back to the kitchen counter and pulled down a large bowl. She added flour and other ingredients, and Beth knew she was about to make the pastry.

Beth thought for a moment. Would adding just one apple pie be enough? "It's the day the stage comes through," she suddenly announced for Wyatt's benefit. "Until they arrive, we won't know how many there are."

Martha grimaced. "Surely they can tell you how many people are on the stage? You've had to guess at the numbers for how long?" Her hands on her hips, Martha seemed determined. "Wyatt, maybe you can convince the stage office to hand over those details."

He didn't hesitate. "I'll be back shortly," he said, determination written all over his face. "Hopefully with the details you need." He stormed out the door, and Beth knew he would do his best to help.

"I'll make the pie anyway," Martha said. "If not tonight, it will be fine for tomorrow. We can make it the day's special," she said, grinning across at her friend. Suddenly, her mood changed. "Right. Now that Wyatt is gone, tell me what's really going on." Hands to her hips, Beth knew her friend meant business.

Beth wasn't sure she wanted to answer and shook her head. Martha moved to her side and put an arm around her. "I'm torn," Beth whispered. "I'm falling for Wyatt, but I feel…" she took a deep breath and let it out slowly. "I feel loyalty to Joe."

She enjoyed the comfort from her friend, but wasn't sure she wanted to hear the words she knew were coming. "Joe has been dead for a little over eight years now. Look at me, Beth," she said, and gently held her friend's chin and turned her to face her. "He would not want you to angst over this. And he certainly wouldn't want you to be lonely. You're still a young woman. Wyatt is a wonderful man, and he loves you."

Overcome with emotion, Beth didn't answer for some time. Instead, she turned away from Martha. "I know," she whispered. "But I still feel guilty. I loved Joe, I really did. It doesn't seem right to love another man."

"The part that says *until death do we part* is what you need to remember. Joe is dead. Wyatt is alive and kicking." Martha pulled her closer and hugged her tight. Beth knew her friend was right. It was what she'd been fighting with herself. "You're still young. Maybe not spring chicken young, but you're certainly not old." Martha laughed then, and Beth couldn't help but laugh too.

"If I'm young enough to marry again, then so are you," Beth said. "Perhaps Dennis might fix you up with a husband as well."

Martha rolled her eyes. "Don't even think about it. I'd best get back to work." She glanced up as the front door opened. "Wyatt's back. Did you find anything out?" She shouted the last sentence.

"I did indeed. There will be eight passengers, plus two staff to feed. From now on, you can get those numbers on request." He winked then and grinned. "It pays to know people in high places."

Without thinking, Beth stepped forward and hugged him. "Thank you, Wyatt. I appreciate it, I really do." His arms came up around her as Beth had hoped, and she didn't try to move out of his embrace. She was enjoying the comfort of his arms, but knew she was getting far too used to it. Far too familiar with the sheriff. All that said, she did not regret the fact she'd kissed the sheriff.

"Are we ready?" Beth asked as the time got nearer for their transient customers to arrive. She glanced about the diner—everything appeared to be in order. Still, she had the feeling something was amiss, but couldn't fathom what that might be.

Martha was well organized, which was nothing new, and had the plates ready. The stagecoach passengers would pay their own way, but the stage office would pay for their staff. There was nowhere else in town for them to eat except the bakery, and they didn't serve substantial meals. It was a lot of work, especially not knowing numbers, but Wyatt had fixed that problem for her.

It was then Beth understood what was missing. Only it wasn't a *what*, it was *who*. Wyatt was not there, and his presence was sorely missed. In a mere day, she had become so used to having him there by her side. That was fine for now, but moving forward a week, and he would be back at his usual job of being the town sheriff. The thought sent daggers through her heart.

The door suddenly opened, Wyatt at the helm. He always vetted passengers as they left the stagecoach, and today was no different, despite him being on leave. Wyatt told them he wouldn't risk criminals coming into the diner, so he went to scrutinize each passenger for himself.

Beth hurried into the dining area and guided passengers to tables. A young couple wanted to eat alone. The staff sat at another table together, and the remaining passengers shared a table. It didn't bother Beth, provided they all behaved. Knowing the sheriff was nearby, she was certain they would.

"There is roast lamb with roasted vegetables, as well as chicken pot pie," she told each table of customers. She left them alone for a few minutes before taking their orders, then returned to the kitchen. The majority went for the roast, which is what she expected. Wyatt helped Martha carry the meals out, since Beth was not capable of doing it one-handed.

It wasn't long before Martha was preparing for the second course. Wyatt helped with drinks, and that was also a great help. With apple pie and cherry cobbler sliced up ready to serve, all they needed was to know who wanted what. There was plenty to go around, provided everyone didn't all choose the same dessert.

One problem Beth had encountered in the past was passengers not paying as they left the diner. Wyatt had promised to ensure that didn't happen, and she knew he would be true to his word. She could never understand why anyone would believe it was alright to steal from the diner in this way.

After supper was over, and everyone had eaten their fill, Wyatt took his place at the front counter. He put on his ferocious sheriff's face, and it was all Beth could do not to laugh. She didn't lose the cost of a single meal. She wondered if Wyatt was willing to do that as a side-line job. It would be worth every cent it cost her.

Once the diner was empty, the passengers hurried back to the stagecoach. They had a bit of time before the stage left, but not a lot. This time around, no one was staying permanently in town. Which wasn't unusual. Crystal Springs was small compared to most of the other towns out this way.

"Thank you, Wyatt," Beth said, coming up beside him. "I usually lose at least the cost of two meals each time the stage comes through."

Wyatt frowned. "From now on, I'll ensure they all pay in advance. Or I'll be here to ensure that doesn't happen."

Good on Wyatt. He was always thinking about her, but she couldn't expect him to be here and control payments each time the stage came through. Besides, sometimes he had sheriff's business to deal with. Beth shook her head. "I can't ask you to do that. I'm sure we can work something out."

"Beth," he said, staring down into her face. "You didn't ask. I offered. I will not abide anyone stealing in my town. Especially not from my girl." He winked at her, and a thrill ran from her head to her toes. Was she his girl? They had not discussed such a thing. They weren't exactly courting. Or were they?

She shook herself mentally. No, they weren't courting. At least not to her knowledge. Of course, she was the one who started all this…nonsense. Kissing Wyatt was not her best moment, although he seemed to think it was. But then again, there was a time he thought it was a truly bad idea. Confusion overcame her. "Are we courting?"

Wyatt studied her this time. "Is that a problem? I kind of thought we were." His eyes never left hers, and he continued to stare, perhaps waiting for an answer.

Chapter Eleven

"There's still plenty of food, so let's eat," Martha said as she walked into the dining room. Then she stopped. "What's going on?" she asked tentatively.

Wyatt glanced up at her. She might have saved Beth from giving an answer right this moment, but it was something he and Beth would have to sit down and discuss.

"Nothing to worry about," Beth said, then glanced his way. She then headed toward the kitchen, snatching up his hand on her way.

He enjoyed the warmth of Beth's hand in his, and enjoyed her company—very much. Their relationship, their situation, was still up in the air, and until they had that conversation, things would remain the same.

"There's plenty of roast, as well as chicken pot pie," Martha announced. Then she stood back and stared at them both. "I know something is going on, so you might as well tell me."

Wyatt's heart thudded. He wasn't sure he wanted to discuss his private business with Martha, even if she was Beth's friend.

"I'll tell you later," Beth said, then glanced his way. "Let's just eat now."

"Of course," Martha said, then pierced Wyatt with her eyes. What did she think he'd done?

There was still enough of both main meals to go around, and he opted for the roast. Martha filled his plate, but her piercing gaze told Wyatt she was far from happy.

Heck, he was not happy. Why he even expected anything to come from Beth's advances, he didn't know. They'd been friends for far too long to allow themselves to become more involved. But they did, and now they both had to live with the consequences. The worst part of all was walking away. Now he'd got to know Beth better, he wanted to learn even more about her.

Was he being selfish? Sitting at the table in the dining area, he glanced across at her as they ate. It was clear Martha knew something was afoot, and continued to give him the cold shoulder. He liked

Beth's friend, always had. Although he didn't like the way she interfered with their relationship. It was not Martha's business.

"Alright," Martha suddenly said as she threw her knife and fork onto the table. "What is going on? You could cut the air with a knife." Again, she pierced Wyatt with her eyes, and it made him want to slink down into the chair and under the table.

Beth stared at Wyatt, then Martha. Was she going to reveal their private conversation to her friend? "I…" Her gaze went back to Wyatt, and it stayed there. "Wyatt called me *his girl*."

A slow smile crossed Martha's lips. "Wonderful," she said, then clapped her hands together.

"No, it's not!" Beth said between gritted teeth. "We're not courting."

"She's right, we're not," Wyatt said. "But I would be honored if we were."

Instead of smiling as he thought she would, Beth continued to glare at him. Martha was smiling, which was predictable, given their conversations of late. "Then make it official," Martha said. "There's no reason not to." She lifted her cutlery and began eating again.

Beth glared at Martha, then at Wyatt. His heart pounded, and he wasn't sure what to expect next.

"Alright, I supposed we can court," Beth said, albeit reluctantly.

On the one hand, Wyatt was ecstatic. On the other hand, she'd said it grudgingly. He would have to prove to her he was worth the effort.

He smiled at her, then reached for her hand and squeezed it. Then he continued to eat as though something life-changing had not just occurred.

After helping Martha clean up the kitchen, and then the dining room, Wyatt offered to escort both the women home. They both refused. However, he wasn't one to be deterred, especially since it was already twilight. Instead, he insisted on escorting. Martha first, and then he took Beth to her house, which wasn't much further.

He'd never visited Beth at her home before, and until tonight, didn't know exactly where she lived. It wasn't as though Crystal Springs was huge; it was because Wyatt always saw her either at the diner or the mercantile. He had kept his distance all this time because he knew exactly how things would go once he let his feelings known.

As predicted, he was right.

"Goodnight, Martha," Wyatt said, almost at the same moment Beth said it. They both stared at each other, then laughed. Martha said nothing, but the smug look on her face said it all. They were like two peas in a pod, and they all knew it.

"Goodnight, you two," she said. "I'll see you at the diner in the morning, Beth."

Wyatt studied her before speaking. "I'll be there, too," he said. "You can't get rid of me that quickly." He chuckled then, but Martha didn't laugh. Neither did Beth.

"You don't have to help. I won't hold you to it," Beth told him. Instead of answering, Wyatt patted her hand. The same hand that was hooked through his arm, and gave him a warm feeling that seemed to flow through his entire body.

"I want to help. Besides," he said, revelling in the warmth of her skin, "there are still lots of repairs that need to be dealt with. Not only in the kitchen, but around the property." Surely she wouldn't deny him the opportunity to make something good out of an unpleasant situation?

She nodded then, but seemed to stiffen in his hold. "I appreciate it. I really do. Provided it doesn't cause problems for you with your job."

It was sweet of Beth to think that way, but he had no concerns in that area. He hadn't missed even one day since taking over as sheriff two years ago and was certainly entitled to this short amount of time off. "I won't get into trouble, if that's what you think." He watched her carefully, and she seemed to squirm under his scrutiny.

Instead of answering, she pointed to the cottage ahead of them. "This is me," she whispered, although Wyatt did not know why she dropped her voice so low. There were no houses right next to hers, so they wouldn't disturb any close neighbors, since there were none.

Beth took a key out of her reticule and went to unlock the door. "Let me do that for you," Wyatt said, then cupped her hand in both his. A thrill ran through him. It was not a sensation he had experienced before, and it confused him momentarily. Then he glanced down at their entwined hands and understood completely. How he had allowed their distant friendship to linger for so long, he had no idea. Wyatt understood it was his own fault. He'd kept Beth at a distance all this time for his own selfish reasons.

Being a confirmed bachelor all these years was a choice. It might not have been the best option, but having a dangerous occupation was not something he longed to share with the woman he loved.

Finally, Wyatt had acknowledged his love for Beth, even if they both tried to deny it. The problem was, they were both set in their ways. It meant neither of them really wanted to start a relationship that may not survive. When you got to be their age, it was not so easy.

Wyatt studied her in the moonlight, just as he had around this time last night. As it did the previous night, the moon shone down onto her face. Beth stared up at him, likely waiting for him to unlock the door. He felt like an awkward teenager right this moment, fumbling with the key, trying to get it in the lock.

"Here, let me," Beth said, and took the key from his fingers. When she turned the key, the door swung open, and she stepped inside. "Goodnight, Wyatt," she said, glancing up at him.

"Goodnight, Beth," he said, and turned away. She was about to close the door when he turned back.

"Is everything alright," she asked, confusion on her face.

"I forgot something," he whispered, then took Beth in his arms and kissed her. She didn't resist, didn't fight, so he continued until they were both breathless. "I think I should go," he said, then hurried away.

Wyatt did not turn back to check Beth's reaction, but she didn't complain, so he headed home with a smile on his face.

Chapter

Twelve

Beth glanced up when Wyatt strolled into the diner as though nothing was amiss.

Her fingers went to her lips with the memory of last night's kiss. The lingering touch of his lips on hers had stayed with her all night, and Beth had barely slept. This morning, she felt like a wreck. The dark circles under her eyes were testament to her lack of sleep.

"Good morning," Wyatt said with a grin on his face. Martha spun around to face them both, her eyes piercing. They'd been friends for far too long, and Martha could read her like a book. A slow smile crossed her lips.

"Good morning," Martha said, in a sing-song way.

Beth stared at Wyatt, and his eyes seemed to sparkle, but he had the same tell-tale signs of lost sleep she had—dark circles under his eyes.

"What am I doing today?" Wyatt asked, then, before Beth could answer, went back to the shelf. The one that caused all the upset the previous day. He wiggled it about for a moment, then opened his toolbox and, securing the correct tool for the job, removed the shelf completely.

Beth's breath whooshed out of her mouth. She felt a weight lift from her shoulders, which was the strangest feeling.

Martha was next to her before Beth knew what was happening. Wyatt studied her and only continued when Martha nodded.

It didn't hit Beth immediately. She couldn't fathom what was going on, but apparently her two friends did. She glanced across at Wyatt and saw the shelf in his hands. The shelf her dead husband had installed all those years ago.

The simple action of removing a shelf was her last connection with the husband she had loved dearly.

Wyatt's sad eyes continued to study her. Then, without a word, he placed the discarded shelf inside the cupboard below. Out of her sight. But not out of her memory.

Suddenly, the room was filled with movement. Martha went back to the stove, and Wyatt was studying the wall and taking measurements.

"Breakfast is ready," Martha announced, and while she still felt as though she was in a stupor, Beth was guided to a table. "Have some tea," her friend told her. "You'll feel better."

Her breakfast was placed in front of her, and Beth glanced up to see Wyatt towering over her. She loved the fact her friends rallied around her when she needed them, but left her alone when that was what she needed.

Right now, she welcomed their friendly faces and kind words. Today was the end of an era for Beth. She had vowed to move forward. After being a widow for so many years, it was time to live again. Hadn't Martha had told her this very thing for years now? She couldn't continue to mourn a husband who had been dead longer than they'd been married. It was a fact she had to finally accept.

She lifted the mug to her lips and sipped the steaming hot beverage. Wyatt sat opposite and studied her, trying not to let it show. She wanted to laugh, but didn't want to offend him. Right now, though, she needed happiness. Beth felt torn, despite Wyatt removing the last vestige of her husband.

Still, it could take some time. Surely it would. Relief like that couldn't be instantaneous. Although she felt an instant reprieve, now she felt guilty. It was like that when Joe was killed. They were crossing the road together. Beth was mere steps ahead of him and turned at the sound of the wagon pummelling down on them. Her memory of that day still kept her awake at night.

Beth shook herself mentally. She couldn't continue to feel guilt over something she had no control over.

"How is your arm today?" Wyatt's voice pulled her out of her worst nightmare. Had he guessed where her thoughts were headed?

"Not as bad as I expected," she said, then went back to eating her oats.

Martha placed a plate of biscuits in the middle of the table, then joined them. "Everything fine? Food to your liking?" she asked, a smile on her face. Neither Beth nor Wyatt would complain, and they all knew it. Wyatt, for once, was eating properly.

Beth knew he went to the bakery for pastries in the early hours occasionally. There wasn't much that went on in this town without everyone hearing about it. The thought made her wince. Would the word about them courting get around as quickly? No doubt it would. At least for now, they had only spoken about courting. Nothing had made it real.

When things got real, the entire population of Crystal Springs would be filled with gossip about the sheriff and the widow from the diner.

"Everything is in hand here," Martha announced once breakfast was over and she was preparing for lunch. "Why don't you two go for a stroll… or whatever it is you do when courting?" She had a sly smile on her face, and Beth knew she wanted to get things moving between her and Wyatt.

"That sounds like a great idea. I'm already missing my nightly strolls when I do my rounds." He patted his belly. "I don't want to put on weight. Mind you, I'm being so well fed here, it's bound to happen." He laughed, and the women joined him. Wyatt was such a wonderful man, and she couldn't fathom why she had waited so long to move their relationship forward.

It had been clear to Beth for a considerable time they were compatible. Wyatt being Wyatt, it was obvious he would not make a move, so it had to come from her.

Her mind went back to that moment. Was it really only two days ago? She shook herself mentally. A lot had happened in that short time. As much as the accident was terrible, it was the catalyst for change. She couldn't complain about that. Right now, they were on the cusp of what could be a life-changing situation.

Even if it wasn't, they gave it a shot. She couldn't ask for more than that.

"Do you need any supplies?" she suddenly asked Martha. "I can get them before we go."

Wyatt came up behind her. "I'll get whatever is needed. How are you going to carry supplies back to here?" He grinned at her, and Beth knew he was joking with her. Wyatt seemed to come out of his shell since he'd been helping at the diner. She liked the old Wyatt, but she liked the new Wyatt even more.

In many ways, this really had been good. She'd got to know Wyatt, the man, rather than the sheriff. Why she'd left it this long, she didn't know. Except, deep down, she did. There was never an opportunity to spend time with him one-on-one. There were always customers around, or they'd see each other at the mercantile or elsewhere in town. It had taken all her courage to invite Wyatt to supper the other night. She hadn't planned on kissing him, but when the opportunity arose…who was she to deny the moment?

Martha studied them both. "Supplies are fine. Just go, both of you." She waved them out of the diner, as though her life depended on it.

"I think we got kicked out of my diner!" Beth said, pretending to be appalled.

Wyatt laughed. "I think you're right, but it doesn't bother me. What about you?" he asked, staring down into her face.

"Not even one iota." She smiled then, and he reached for her hand. "Where shall we go?" Beth asked.

"Assuming we don't have a lot of time, why don't we go to the park? It's peaceful there."

Warmth flooded Beth. "It's nice there. I rarely go to the park as I don't like to go alone." She thought about the number of times she felt vulnerable walking home late at night, let alone being out during the day without an escort.

"I can't imagine," Wyatt said gently. "That stops now. And from now on, you don't walk home alone at night." He shook his head. "I'm sorry, Beth. I am a fool. I should never have allowed you to walk from the diner by yourself at night." He scowled then. "I don't know what I was thinking."

She glanced up at him. Wyatt was a big man, well over six feet tall. And he was solid. No one in their right mind would tackle him. No wonder she felt protected when he was around. Was that all it was between them? Did she feel toward him as a protector, or was there more to it? The last thing

Beth wanted was to lead Wyatt on. To make him think she was in love with him when she truly wasn't would be a cruel and ugly trick.

Her heart thudded. She needed to sort out the truth and act on it. Sooner rather than later.

Chapter Thirteen

Sitting next to Beth in the gazebo was nice.

If he was truthful, it was more than nice—it was the best feeling and he didn't want it to end. The sun was shining, and it was a pleasant day. Being here with Beth made it even better. If he was not on leave and was doing his regular job, Wyatt would likely be filling out paperwork back at the office.

It wasn't his favorite thing to do; this was far more fun. He reached for Beth's hand and gently squeezed it. She seemed surprised at his touch. "I didn't mean to startle you," Wyatt said, and let go of her hand.

She turned to face him. "I was thinking. My mind was elsewhere." She reached across and held his hand then, and a shiver went down his spine.

"What do you want, Beth?" he suddenly asked. It probably wasn't a fair question, given they were not as familiar with each other as he'd like. Instead of answering, she stared at him. "Where do you want this to go? With us, I mean?" She'd instigated this whole thing, so it would help to know what she really wanted.

"I…uh," she stammered. He'd taken her off guard, which probably wasn't a bad thing. With criminals, Wyatt found that was the best way to get information. But this was Beth, the woman he loved with all his heart.

"It's alright," Wyatt said. "You don't have to answer." He turned away then, annoyed with himself for putting her in an awkward position.

"What I want," Beth said forcefully, "is to be with someone I love. I need to know that person loves me back, and does not feel pressured into saying they love me when they don't." She took a deep breath and let it out slowly. "Do you love me, Wyatt? Because I think I love you."

His heart twisted. She only thought she loved him? He guessed that was a start. He loved her dearly, even if he hadn't told her so. "I do love you, Beth. I think I've loved you from that first day—when I arrived in town, and you took me under your wing, feeding me when you thought I needed it." He couldn't help but grin. Except Beth didn't smile. In fact, she turned away. "Beth?" He gently turned her head to face him. "I understand how difficult this must be for you. I know you still grieve your husband. I didn't know him, but I'm told he was a wonderful man."

Her eyes filled with tears. "He certainly was. Joe was a dutiful husband and would have been a wonderful father. He died far too soon." Wyatt pulled Beth close and wrapped his arms around her. It seemed obvious they wouldn't have the chance to court unless that part of her life was behind her. Clearly it wasn't. "I'm sorry," she said, wiping at her eyes. "Joe is long gone, and I need to move forward."

The one thing he longed to hear but didn't, was Beth's declaration of love. Did that mean she'd changed her mind? After all, it was Beth who kissed him first. It was she who started this entire scenario. His heart felt as though it was being squeezed in a vice, to the point he couldn't breathe. Still, he understood. It was a big change, and he had to give her time to adjust. If that was what she wanted.

"Beth," Wyatt said, gently pushing her away so he could glance into her face. "I love you dearly, but you're not ready. For me, it's all or nothing. I've never been married, but I was engaged once. I know what it's like to lose someone you love." She stared at him in disbelief. "I'll be here when you want me. Until then, I think it's better that I keep away." His heart felt as though it was shattering into a million pieces, but he wouldn't be with someone against their will.

All color drained from Beth's face. "I'm sorry," she whispered.

Wyatt stood then and helped Beth to her feet. The walk back to the diner was in silence. He opened the door for her, then walked away. Putting one foot after another, leaving Beth behind, was the most difficult thing he'd done in his entire life.

"You're like a bear with a sore head," Tommy said. "Go back to your girlfriend."

Wyatt glared at his deputy. "What's it to you?" he growled, which was so unlike him. Wyatt never yelled or growled at anyone. Especially not people he admired. He might occasionally let his guard down with criminals, but that was it.

Two days aways from Beth, and it felt like weeks. Until he spent his days in the diner, Wyatt didn't realize exactly how much he really loved her. Two years of keeping his distance was difficult, but these past two days away from her were excruciating. "I apologize," he said, then shoved his chair back and stormed out of the office.

Probably not his best moment, but his pent up anger at himself was not helping. It was his fault, and his fault alone, that he was no longer courting Beth. It must have been the shortest period of courting on record.

Glancing down the street, he spotted Beth coming out of the diner. She was heading toward the mercantile. He should go there. She would need someone to carry the supplies back to the diner. She certainly couldn't do it, not with one arm.

As though she sensed his presence, Beth glanced down the street and suddenly her gaze was trained in his direction. He closed his eyes momentarily. Wyatt vowed he would not be the first to make a move. He told Beth he'd give her time, and he would do exactly that. It might be extremely difficult, but he would push through.

She turned to face him. Her uninjured arm went up. "Wyatt," she called, a smile on her face. His heart pounded. Was Beth reaching out to him? Or was it only his imagination?

She strolled toward him, then her pace got quicker. He couldn't very well refuse when she reached out, could he?

"Beth," he said with a sigh as he walked close to her. Why did his heart betray him? *I've missed you,* he almost said, but kept the words to himself.

"Do you have a minute to help? I have to collect some stores. Martha is too busy right now to help."

Her words shattered his hopes. What she wanted was his muscle power. What she didn't want was Wyatt, and that cut right through his entire being.

"Of course," he said, ensuring he didn't give away his true feelings. "Anything for you." The moment he uttered the last words, Wyatt knew he should have kept them to himself. "How have you been?" he asked as they strolled toward the mercantile together.

He reached forward and opened the door for Beth. She turned back and glanced at him. Biting back a smile, she nodded. Were they less than friends now? His heart broke all over again.

"Good morning, you lovebirds," Dennis said as they entered. He rubbed his hands together, and Wyatt groaned.

"We don't need a running commentary," Wyatt snapped.

Beth's head quickly turned his way. Her hand went to his arm. "Are you alright?" she whispered as she pulled him away from the counter.

He stared into her eyes—he always could get lost in those soulful brown eyes. "No, I'm not," he said, then moved back to the counter. "I apologize, Dennis," he said.

Thankfully, Beth handed him her shopping list and diverted the uncomfortable conversation.

"Hopefully, you have everything on the list. Do you know when my regular order is arriving?"

Wyatt knew Beth was trying to keep the conversation on business rather than let Dennis bring it back to a personal level, and for that, he was grateful.

Dennis scanned the list. "I have no idea, sorry. On a better note, I have supplies of everything on this list. Give me ten or fifteen minutes, and I'll have it ready for you."

Great. That meant he had to spend even more time with Beth. Not that he didn't want to be with her, but until she was clear about what she wanted, he had planned to keep away. That didn't include not being there to help when necessary.

"We'll wait outside," Beth said. "I need some fresh air."

Dennis had already begun to pull the order together, and Wyatt hoped that meant it wouldn't be too long. They headed out and sat on the wooden bench near the store. "Are you alright?" he asked. She was far too pale for his liking. "You don't look well."

Beth studied him. "My arm has been giving me some trouble these past couple of days."

Her statement took his breath away. "I'm taking you to the doc. He can check it out." He stood then, ready to go this very moment.

"I…I have to get the supplies. Martha needs them." Beth's objection was frustrating, but he could see her point.

"As soon as I've delivered them to the diner, we're off to have that arm checked." This time, she nodded. Beth knew he had her best interests at play, and her health was important. Funny how literally days changed his entire life.

Instead of being selfish and self-centred as he had been for years, he worried about someone else. Not just anyone, but a particular other person. Wyatt sat back down. He'd hoped they could talk, but neither of them said another word until Dennis tapped on the window. "You stay here, I've got this," Wyatt said.

It wasn't long before they entered the diner and he delivered the box of supplies to the kitchen. Martha turned around to face him. "Thank you, Wyatt," she said, with a smug look on her face. There was something about Martha he admired, and that was her ability to openly let everyone know what she was thinking. She never tried to hide anything, and her facial expressions said it all.

This time she was telling him it was about time he returned. Without uttering a single word. He knew she was right, but unless Beth told him otherwise, he would keep away. "Unless there's something else, I'm taking Beth to the doctor." He ushered her out the door.

"Wait! What? Has something happened?" Martha was suddenly concerned.

Beth stared at her friend. "I'm fine. It's just Wyatt being overprotective."

Wyatt grimaced. Isn't that what he was supposed to do? Make sure she was protected and fine? He was confused now. He honestly believed that was his job as her friend. "Her arm is painful today. I'm getting it checked out."

Martha raised her eyebrows and studied Beth. "You didn't tell him?" She faced Wyatt then. "It was giving her trouble yesterday, too. After she pulled the large pot from the cupboard. I tried to stop her…" Martha said, her voice trailing off.

If he'd been around, he would have done it for her. "You've probably torn your stitches," Wyatt said, trying not to sound frustrated. It didn't work. "Come on, the sooner we get there, the better."

Chapter Fourteen

Doctor Marcus Ryan glared at Wyatt. "How did you let this happen? I told you both that arm had to be rested. It is very clear that wasn't the case." He shook his head, then turned away.

Beth felt fully admonished.

"I'm sorry, Doc. I should have ensured your instructions were followed." Wyatt grimaced as he gazed down at her gaping arm. It was red and nasty looking, and it was all Beth could do not to turn away. "I guess this is going to extend the recovery time."

"You guessed right, Sheriff. Beth will have an additional week of healing time now that she has torn several stitches." He turned to Beth then. "This time, do what you're told and rest that arm. You, out," he told Wyatt, not even trying to hide his annoyance.

Wyatt stared at her, his entire demeanor appeared defeated. Why he kept blaming himself for the things she did, Beth would never know. This was her fault entirely. She couldn't help herself—she needed to be doing things. While Wyatt was there, he ensured she didn't.

"This is going to hurt," Doc said, then proceeded to add new stitches to her arm. "There is no getting around it, Beth—you'll have a scar." He looked so sad at the prospect, but it didn't bother her. At Beth's age, who would care anyway?

"I'm sorry, Doc. Working is a hard habit to break." She truly was sorry. This time, she would listen to the medical advice she was given. "Don't blame Wyatt. He stopped me at every turn until…" She suddenly stopped talking. Did she really want to tell Doc Ryan about her woes?

The doc studied her. Could he see through her to the pain she was enduring? "What happened?" he asked gently. "I thought you two were getting along fine." Beth's head suddenly shot up. "No sudden movements," he told her, then gazed at her again.

"We were. I…" Beth took a deep breath. "It's Joe. Wyatt says I'm not ready. We broke up." It was all she could do not to cry.

Doc grunted and stopped what he was doing. "Sort it out. Wyatt Holt is a good man. You deserve happiness and so does he." As quickly as he stopped, he began restitching her arm again. "I wish there were some way to isolate your arm to keep you from using it, but there's not." He walked to the door and opened it. "You can come in, Wyatt," Doc said, then began to bandage Beth's arm again.

"What's the verdict, Doc?" Wyatt's concern was clear.

Doc Ryan glanced from one to the other of them. "It's not good. That arm needs to be rested. I'm talking complete rest. No more doing anything, not even lifting a mug of tea." Now he glared at Wyatt. "Is that clear?"

"It's very clear, Doc."

Beth stood. She felt lightheaded and sat down again. She waved Wyatt away when he approached. It was all too much. Not only had she injured herself, now she had a prolonged recovery time. It was completely her own fault.

"I want you to take this Laudanum," Doc said, handing over a bottle. "Instructions are on the label. It's for the pain."

Wyatt hadn't taken his eyes off her since the moment she sat down again. This time, when she tried to stand, an arm went up around her waist.

"Easy," he whispered. "I don't want you to keel over." She stared up into his face. His concern was palpable. It hit her hard.

"I want to check that arm in a few days," Doc called to their retreating backs.

Wyatt handled her like egg shells. He'd always been gentle, but this was a whole new level of tenderness. "Will do, Doc," he called over his shoulder.

Beth breathed in the fresh air when they were outside.

Wyatt stared at her. "Do you need to sit down? Want to go home?" He shook his head then. "I don't know what you need to be comfortable."

Beth leaned into him. "I…" She stared into his face. It was covered in concern for her. For her. Beth's heart pounded. She just wanted to be held in his arms. None of this was Wyatt's fault—it was no one's fault. She didn't blame him, not one iota, but he blamed himself. How could she ease the guilt that engulfed him?

The truth was, she couldn't. All she could do was carry on the way she'd already done. Easing his guilt was impossible. That had already been proven time and time again. "Wyatt?" she whispered. He stared down at her in concern. "I'm sorry—about everything."

"I know," he replied. "I'm sorry too." He wiped a hand across his chin. "You know what? I'm not sorry. I'm not sorry you kissed me, or I kissed you. I'm not sorry for falling in love with you two years ago. I'm not sorry for any of it." Beth stared at him, opened mouthed. "What I am sorry about is that you can't move past the memory of your dead husband." He seemed sad now. "We could have been good together."

He was right. They *were* good together. She was a fool for letting him get away. "I need to sit down," Beth whispered. "Is it too late to try again?" she asked when they were installed on a nearby wooden bench.

Wyatt shook his head. "Is that what you really want? You know how I feel, but that doesn't matter. I won't force you into anything. That's not how I work." She studied him momentarily. Suddenly Wyatt laughed. "Except when it comes to criminals."

It put a smile on her face. That was exactly what Beth needed right now—a reason to smile. She leaned into him and glanced up. "I love you, Wyatt Holt," she whispered, and he leaned down and kissed her.

A lot had happened since the night Beth kissed Wyatt. Not all of it good. Wyatt was determined to put it all behind them.

"What do you think, Doc?" Wyatt asked as Doc Ryan unravelled the bandage on Beth's arm.

The doctor glanced down at her bare arm. "What I think is," he said, staring at the injury, "it appears a lot better. It's only been three days since new stitches were needed, but it looks to be healing well." He redressed the wound and bandaged it again. "I want to check it again in three days."

They were soon on their way again.

Beth sighed. "I'm not sure I can take another three days of this," she said quietly. It was obvious she'd had enough.

Wyatt squeezed her hand. "Which part is the most frustrating for you—resting or doing nothing?" He chuckled, but Beth was far from happy. He could see her frustration every time she wanted to do something and couldn't. He'd been by her side for the most part, but at night, Martha had stayed with Beth. For Wyatt to do so would have been unconscionable. Propriety always had to take precedence, and he understood that.

He had a solution, but Beth rejected it. He would marry her in a heartbeat, but Beth said she didn't want him to feel pressured. As much as he appreciated it, the way he felt hadn't changed.

"Wyatt," Beth said, turning to face him. "Thank you for helping. I know you have to go back to work and understand. You've been so helpful."

Wyatt stiffened. "Who says I'm going back to work? I extended my leave until further notice. This is the first time in the two years since I arrived in Crystal Springs that I've taken time off. The mayor is fine with it, and you should be too." Besides, he was enjoying spending all his days at the diner. Fixing things and helping out was a welcomed change to his usual routine as sheriff. Nothing ever happened here except for the occasional drunk, so it was not a significant issue.

"Oh, Wyatt!" Beth's expression told him she was displeased. Too bad—it wasn't up to her. "We can cope without you. You know that, right?" Her sad puppy dog eyes were almost his undoing.

"Of course I know. But truth be told, it's a pleasant change. I'm enjoying helping out and doing something completely different after all these years." He wanted to add he was certain matchmaker Dennis from the mercantile was enjoying it too, but kept that to himself.

"And the food? I'm sure you're enjoying the food." Beth laughed then, and he was glad to see her smiling. This past week she'd done little of that. Being forced to do nothing didn't sit well with Beth. She was someone who needed to be doing something all the time. Poor Martha had been badgered and annoyed for the entire time Beth was on rest. Luckily, Martha was such a good friend. Anyone else probably wouldn't have put up with it. It made Wyatt smile. "What is so funny?" Beth demanded.

"I was thinking about poor Martha. She must be fed up as well." He grinned then, but Beth pursed her lips. If this was the wrath of Beth, it wasn't too harsh to bear. "Come here," Wyatt said, and pulled her close to him. "We all love you and want the best for you." He held her as tight as he dared, given her current condition.

Beth tipped her head to stare up at him. "I know. I'm bored. I want to do things again." She rested her head against his chest. Wyatt felt warmth fill his very being. This was how he wanted to spend the rest of his days, being close to the woman he loved.

An idea went off in his head. "Beth," he said slowly, quietly. "I need to ask you something." She glanced up at him again and nodded. "You know how much I love you, and you said…"

"I know," she said, confusion written all over her face. "I love you too. There is no doubt in my mind."

By this time, they'd arrived outside the diner, and Wyatt gently pushed her away from him. "Beth," he said in a whisper, then dropped to one knee. "Will you marry me?"

Suddenly, the door opened and Martha stood there gaping at them. "Oooooh," she said, a dreamy look on her face. "Say yes," she instructed her friend, but Beth said not a word.

Disappointment flooded Wyatt. Beth stared at him expectantly. That was when he understood. "I haven't organized a ring yet, but I will. Beth," he said again, "will you marry me?"

His heart pounded, and a shiver ran down his spine. What would he do if she said no? He dreaded the thought.

Beth waved Martha back into the diner. If Wyatt thought his heart couldn't pound any harder, he was wrong. He was sure he would keel over any second when suddenly Beth opened her mouth to speak.

"Wyatt," she said sternly. "I love you to bits, but marry you?" She paused then, and his heart squeezed tightly in his chest. "Of course I'll marry you!"

Suddenly he wasn't sure what to do, but somehow got to his feet and wrapped Beth in his arms, in his warmth, and in his love.

Wyatt couldn't be happier.

They were about to go inside and tell Martha the good news when Dennis called out from across the street. "Congratulations," he said, far more enthusiastically than Wyatt thought he should be. "I was just sweeping the boardwalk," he said, and lifted the broom he held in his hands.

Wyatt eyed him suspiciously. In the two years he'd lived in Crystal Springs, he had never seen Dennis sweep the boardwalk. In fact, he'd never seen him outside his store during the workday. That privilege was reserved for the teenagers he had working part-time for him.

Did that mean Dennis was spying on them? Was he ready to pounce the moment Wyatt looked set to propose? Wyatt swore under his breath.

"Wyatt Holt, you take that back!" Beth was outraged. "You know I don't like that sort of talk."

He looked down at the woman who was soon to be his wife. "My apologies," he said, and truly meant it. "That man is infuriating."

"He really is," Beth said, then slipped her hand in his, and they strolled inside together ready to tell Martha their exciting news.

Less than two weeks later, Wyatt stood at the front of the church, Joel Evans by his side. His friend closed the bakery for the ceremony, as the entire town had done. Despite their wanting a quiet ceremony, word got around quickly. No doubt the work of Dennis Andrews and his well-known penchant for gossip.

Joel tapped him on the shoulder. "She's here," he whispered, then brushed an imaginary spot of fluff from Wyatt's suit. "Are you sure this is what you want?"

Wyatt scowled. "I'm more than sure. I'm absolutely certain. Now stop distracting me from my bride." He turned to face Beth, and what a sight she was. From the moment he'd met her, Wyatt knew she was beautiful. Over time, he'd come to know her beauty was not only on the outside, but on the inside as well.

She stood at the back of the church, and a hush suddenly came over the entire building. Martha stood by her side, fixing her dress, ensuring every inch of her was perfect. Suddenly, the organist began to play, and Beth began the slow walk down the aisle.

Wyatt couldn't help but stare. When she finally arrived at the front of the church to join him, Wyatt reached out for her hand. Warmth flooded him, and simultaneously, his heart flooded. He was so in awe of the woman standing in front of him.

"Who gives this woman away?" Preacher Clyde Walters asked.

Martha stepped forward. "I do," she said, her voice breaking with emotion. Wyatt nodded his thanks to her.

"Do you, Elizabeth Hughes, take this man, Wyatt Holt, to be your lawful wedded husband?" As the preacher continued, Wyatt was mesmerised. He was certain he would be attentive, but found he wasn't. He was enamored with his wife, and didn't want to take his eyes off her. Beth prodded him when it was his turn to answer.

"Ooops, sorry," he whispered. "I do," he told the preacher, his voice far louder this time.

When he slipped the ring on Beth's finger, emotion almost overtook him. Never before in his entire adult life had he loved another person so much.

Wyatt knew they would be together for the rest of their natural lives.

Epilogue

Two years later…

Wyatt watched as Beth gazed down at their baby son. Never did he believe he would become a father, just as Beth told him she'd given up on being a mother.

She'd been barren in her short marriage with Joe, and for several months after their marriage, believed herself to be infertile. Now, watching them both, it was clear she wasn't.

"Wyatt!" Beth quietly called across the room. "Give me your hand."

He hurried across to her and kneeled on the floor next to her chair. She reached out and snatched up his hand. Wonder filled him as he felt his unborn child kicking against his wife's stomach. "It's a miracle," he whispered, not wanting to wake five-month-old Elijah. He stretched himself up and kissed Beth's lips. How he ended up with such a perfect life, he didn't know.

When Beth discovered she was pregnant, Wyatt resigned as sheriff. That was not a risk he was willing to take with his family. They'd already discussed it, even before getting confirmation, and he was eager to walk away.

Helping at the diner had whet his appetite for other endeavors, and left Wyatt wanting for more. Of course, it was highly possible the incentive was being close to Beth. He loved her with all his heart.

Still, that was what he did now, and enjoyed every moment. With his wife busy with Elijah, and another baby on the way, it was impossible for her to run the diner. It was a popular place these days, and far from doing any of the culinary activities, he was there for Martha and her assistant, Allie Hubertson, with whatever they needed. That included Wyatt helping with distributing food when needed, ensuring everything ran smoothly, as well as taking payment as the patrons left.

He also ensured each of the women arrived home safely.

Suddenly, two little eyes opened and glanced up at Beth, and then across at Wyatt. The smile that crossed their son's face filled Wyatt with warmth. If he had known how much joy his little family would bring to his life, Wyatt would have married far earlier.

He thought about that for a moment. A brief moment.

If he'd married previously, he may never have met Beth, who was clearly his soulmate. Nor would Elijah be right here in front of him. Wyatt shook himself mentally. God had a plan for him, and that plan was now in play.

He had lived a long and happy life as a sheriff, and now he was settled and fulfilled. If Beth hadn't invited him to supper that night, if he hadn't asked her to join him on his rounds, and if she hadn't kissed him…

Happily, she did. How different his life, their lives would be right now if none of that had taken place. Hiding his feelings for all that time was the stupidest thing he'd ever done. Thankfully, it was all behind him now, and Wyatt knew they had a long and happy life ahead.

From the Author

Thank you so much for reading my book – I hope you enjoyed it.

I would greatly appreciate you leaving a review where you purchased, even if it is only a one-liner. It helps to have my books more visible!

Multi-published, award-winning and bestselling author Cheryl Wright, former secretary, debt collector, account manager, writing coach, and shopping tour hostess, loves reading.

She writes both historical and contemporary western romance, as well as romantic suspense.

She lives in Melbourne, Australia, and is married with two adult children and has six grandchildren. When she's not writing, she can be found in her craft room making greeting cards.

Website: *http://www.cheryl-wright.com/*

Facebook Reader Group:
https://www.facebook.com/groups/cherylwrightaut hor/

Join My Newsletter:

https://cheryl-wright.com/newsletter/
(and receive a free book)